Two are better than one

Don't do this thing called life alone.

DR. FRANK M. KENDRALLA

This short story is a work of fiction. Any resemblance to persons living or dead is coincidental and is the figment of the character's imagination, and any quote not represented correctly is not done to discredit the author of the quote or public work. The opinions expressed are those of the characters and should not be confused with the author's which at times has an odd sense of humor. Each of us has 1440 minutes per day and must make a choice of how we will invest them in the lives of others and our own.

Two are better than one © by Dr. Frank M Kendralla. All Rights Reserved.

Printed in the United States of America

Published by Author Academy Elite
PO Box 43, Powell, OH 43035
www.AuthorAcademyElite.com

All Rights Reserved. This book contains material protected under International and Federal Copyright Laws and Treaties. Any unauthorized reprint or use of this material is prohibited. No part of this book may be reproduced or transmitted in any form or by any means, electronic or mechanical, including photocopying, recording, or by any information storage and retrieval system, without written permission from the author.

Identifiers:

LCCN: 2019906280
ISBN: 978-1-64085-703-2 (Paperback)
ISBN: 978-1-64085-704-9 (Hardback)
ISBN: 978-1-64085-705-6 (Ebook)
Available in paperback, e-book, and audiobook.

Scripture quotations from The Authorized (King James) Version. Rights in the Authorized Version in the United Kingdom are vested in the Crown. Reproduced by permission of the Crown's patentee, Cambridge University Press

Any internet addresses (websites, blogs, etc.) and telephone numbers printed in this book are offered as a resource. They are not intended in any way to be or imply an endorsement by Author Academy Elite, nor does Author Academy Elite vouch for the content of these sites and numbers for the life of this book

Book design by Jet Launch Cover design by Debbie O'Byrne

DEDICATION

I dedicate this book to my family and every person who takes time to read this book. To my children's children, you made me 'grand' (grandfather). Many people influenced my life, and I hope to explain that you will encounter people in your life that will have a positive impact, and please never forget them! Thank them by saying thank you and by applying what you learn in your life by influencing the lives of others. We all need people, young and old alike, and my intent with this book is to illustrate how people of all ages can impact each of us. Respect and learn from everyone, knowing that "Two are better than one". No one is self-taught, but a product of every person they encounter in their life.

Blessings,

"Dr. Frank"

EPIGRAPH

Two *are* better than one; because they have a good reward for their labour. **Ecclesiastes 4:9**

ACKNOWLEDGMENT

Without my Lord and Saviour, Jesus Christ, this book wouldn't be possible, for, without Him, I know my life wouldn't be the same. Every gift, talent, and ability is a testimony to You, my Lord. My wife of over forty years, Cheryl—A gift—I believe that the statement, iron sharpeneth iron was meant for us. The chemical element for iron—[Fe]male is a perfect illustration of how you sharpened me over our many decades together, and I am a better man because of you.

Countless people influenced my life through books, workshops, webinars, podcasts, school, college, and more. If I included every person, the acknowledgment would be larger than the book. Every word of this book reflects life lessons learned because other people took time for me. Some will state that they are self-made or self-taught. I am the furthest from this mindset. I am a 'noticer' and learn from other people. My desire is for this book to impact the lives of others and emphasize the statement that we need others in our life to learn as we seek guidance and grow in our journey of life.

There are many people I bounced ideas off of and who took the time to read the rough copies, and I thank you from the depth of my heart. Teresa, Amanda, Jean, Ginnie, Stephanie, and Dan are a few who took time from their busy lives to read and provide valuable feedback and encouragement.

Finally, the value my parents played in my life is beyond words, and I cannot thank them enough for the deep-rooted values and love they poured into our lives. Without them, I wouldn't be here writing this acknowledgment and book.

Where no counsel *is*, the people fall: but in the multitude of counsellers *there is* safety. **Proverbs 11:14**

Iron sharpeneth iron; so a man sharpeneth the countenance of his friend. **Proverbs 27:17**

CHAPTER ONE

Tap, tap, tap—

What is that sound? Where am I? Michael thought.

Lifting his head to the sound and through blurry eyes, Michael sees a police officer tapping on his passenger side-window motioning him to open it.

Tap, tap, tap—Shaking his head to clear the fog, Michael reached to turn the ignition.

"Show me your hands and turn the key!" Shouted the officer as he pointed toward the dash.

Getting angrier by the minute, Michael thought, *Stop! I need to turn the vehicle on to put the window down.*

Complying, Michael kept his left hand on the dash and turned the key in the ignition. Then, he pushed the button to open the passenger side window, stopping halfway.

"Open the window all the way!" the officer shouted as he points down and motions toward Michael.

"Sir, what did I do?" Michael said in as calm of a voice as he could while feeling the sweat trickle down his back and his ears turned red with anger filling his body.

The officer responded, "We received multiple calls from residents stating there is a guy parked in a large black SUV with tinted windows that they don't recognize. Hand me your ID, vehicle registration, and insurance card, and open the window all the way."

While reaching in his suit jacket to retrieve his wallet, the wallet fell to the floor between his feet.

As he reached toward the floor to retrieve the wallet, Michael wondered what else could go wrong today.

"Stop! Don't do anything else except get out of your vehicle! Now!"

While struggling to get out of the vehicle, Michael's foot caught, causing him to stumble forward nearly doing a face plant on the ground.

"Are you drunk!" the officer said as he put his hand on his gun holster. "Your eyes are bloodshot, and you can't stand up."

"No," he said, and then he paused. "Sir, I don't drink. I had a horrible week and Abby—never mind. I don't drink."

"Stand at the back of the vehicle and don't move!" The officer stooped down, retrieving Michael's wallet from the floor without taking his eyes off him.

"I will give you a sobriety test and check your information," said the officer as he handed the wallet to Michael.

"Is your license and registration in your wallet?"

"Yes."

"Remove them from your wallet and slowly hand them to me."

What a week! Michael sighed as he handed his information to the officer.

Where am I? Abby and I had a horrible fight. Was it last night? Was it two days ago? In all of our years of marriage, I don't think we ever said the things we said.

Michael's mind raced back to the previous few weeks as he recalled the night that led him to drive away from his home and family at breakneck speed until he couldn't drive anymore. He had pulled over and fallen asleep near a community just off the interstate.

He remembered having an argument with his boss, going home, then having the worst fight of his life with Abby, his wife of twelve years. He stormed out of the house crying, screaming at the top of his lungs while his three little children cried while clinging to her legs. He doesn't

CHAPTER ONE

remember how long he drove, but he knew he was speeding the entire time.

I do not understand how I wasn't stopped for speeding or worse. I remember nodding off and deciding to stop to rest but . . .

Michael snapped to the present when the officer shouted, "Mister–are you listening to me? I told you to walk this line."

Thirty minutes later, after a series of sobriety tests, the officer handed the keys and information back to Michael.

In a calm voice, the officer said. "Young man, what is wrong?"

Surprised by the change in tone from the officer, Michael thought, *Young man? Why the change in attitude?*

After studying the officer for a few minutes, he thought, *How old is he, fifty or sixty but he is fit, and I wouldn't want to fight him. I wouldn't want to fight anyone. There is something about his eyes, they are dazzling and bright.*

Hesitating, Michael said, "Nothing."

Then, out of character, emotion overtook him as he cried and sat on the curb, putting his face in his hands, sobbing like a child.

After a few minutes, the officer said, "Michael, my name is Officer Dan. I'm letting you off with a warning for parking illegally in a residential no-parking area. My shift ends in 30 minutes, and I need to write this up. If you'd like, I can buy you breakfast at the diner a few miles from here, and we can talk, guy to guy."

"Thank you," Michael said, surprised at the offer. "Yes, I can meet you there for a chat. That would be great. I am famished, and some food will help."

Officer Dan gave Michael the address of the diner and his private mobile number. A few minutes later, Michael arrived at the diner.

This reminds me of the small town featured in the T.V. show my nana and I watched years ago, thought Michael as a smile formed on his face and he almost laughed out loud.

Those were the carefree days when she would tickle my face, and we would laugh and hug, and I would play like I didn't like it then say, "More—more." Why was life so difficult now? What happened to the carefree days, and how did Abby and I end up hating each other one minute then loving each other the next?

Looking around, Michael thought, *where am I? Where is the officer, I thought he would be here by now. I hope he isn't like all of other older men in my life who lectured me, telling me to suck it up buttercup and deal with life like a man.*

Every guy in his life told him the same thing repeating standard guy clichés. Work hard and make hay when the sun shined. Daily, he went to a high-paying job he despised to give his family all the things he thought they wanted.

His wife didn't need to work, and he made more than his dad many times over while driving a car that most families could not afford while living in one of the most affluent neighborhoods around. Yes, they were up to their ears in debt, combined with him working fourteen plus hour days six to seven days per week, it had all lead up to the fight, but . . .

He was brought back to the present when Officer Dan called his name.

"Michael, let's go inside. I know the folks who own this café, and they make the best food in the county."

When they walked in, Officer Dan was greeted by chorus of—"Good morning, Officer Dan." A plump little lady only five feet tall came to him and gave him a huge hug, nearly lifting the over six-foot tall 185-pound man off the ground.

"Glad to see you, son. Who's your friend?"

The sweet aroma of maple syrup, pancakes, and potatoes filled the air.

After a quick introduction, they headed to a hand made wood and padded booth in the back of the diner, which was unlike the other booths and tables that resembled what was

CHAPTER ONE

found in most eateries. It was then that Michael noticed the diner's name on a sign on the back inside wall.

"Nana's Place. If you leave hungry, it's your own fault, not mine! But we still love you." Michael relaxed as he recalled a saying his nana often said, "Love you mostest. Said it first, mean it most."

They ordered, and the server brought two large plates of potatoes, eggs, peppers, onions, avocados, fruit, and a massive pot of coffee. The coffee's smell filled his nostrils, sending a jolt of energy from its fragrance, which wasn't flowery.

"Michael, have you called your wife to let her know you are okay?" Officer Dan asked.

With a mouth full of food, Michael attempted to respond but shook his head no.

In a soft tone, Officer Dan said, "I suggest at least sending her a text message to let her know you are okay and that you will call her later. She deserves the peace of mind that you didn't do something foolish, putting you and your family at risk. I am sure she is worried about you."

At this comment, Michael rolled his eyes, puts down his fork, and dug his phone from his suit pocket, realizing that even a text message could start a conversation with Abby he wasn't ready to have. After sending a short text message to his wife telling her he was okay and would call her later, he turned off his phone, and put it in his suit jacket's inside pocket.

"Michael, what is it you do, and do you have a dream? I mean, a real dream for your life. Not the dream of others for your life but a dream that causes you to lie awake at night that excites you beyond anything imaginable. And you know that if you achieved this dream, you could be the change the world needs, or at least give your world what it needs?"

With a mouth half full of food, Michael said in a sarcastic tone, "I'm living the dream."

He added under his breath, "I'm a VP for a marketing firm."

CHAPTER TWO

Abby read the text message from Michael for the third time. "I am fine and will call you later."

In all of their years together, regardless of how bad the fight was, he always ended with 'LuvUtoo.'

After receiving the text, she tried to call him, but the call went to voice mail. She sent a simple text—"I love you forever and a day."

Yes, their fight was one of the worst, if not the worst ever and after Michael left, she fell asleep with all three kids huddled tight to her, listening to their sobs come and go throughout the night. She felt horrible knowing she needed to say what she said, but maybe if her delivery were different, Michael would have received it better.

At least she knew he was okay and didn't end up in an accident. Michael was a good man, hardworking, and a good provider, but at the rate he was going, he wouldn't make it to his 40th birthday. She couldn't just stand by and say nothing. She loved him so much there were times it hurt.

Knowing Michael was okay, she needed to get the three kids cleaned up and do something to get her mind off last night's argument. She called her three-time divorced friend, Stella. Abby wanted to head to the gym and spa to burn off some energy and frustration. However, before she called Stella, she sent a text to Jasmine, the teen she often used to watch the kids when 'girl time' was needed and set the time for Jasmine to come to the house.

CHAPTER THREE

"Michael, Michael . . ." Officer Dan repeated a few times. "Are you ok?"

"Yes, well, no. I am not living the dream, nor do I know how to live the dream in my heart," replied Michael in a soft and cracking voice as if he would break down and cry again.

Just then the server returned and filled their coffee cups, asking, "Do you want some fresh made Apple Pie? Nana made a few pies from the apples Pete brought over earlier in the week, and if I do say so myself, this is the best pie she made all week." In a hushed tone, the server said, "Don't tell Nana I said this but don't eat the 'healthy' version - those gluten-free pies she made, I don't think the stray animals would eat."

Officer Dan had to hold in his laughter and responded while pretending to zip his lips shut with his right hand, "My lips are sealed, and yes we will each have a piece of Nana's pie with a scoop of ice cream from Polly's dairy."

The server cleared a few of their plates and was off to fetch their pies.

"Michael, when we are done here, I would like to introduce you to a few friends in the community, if it's okay with you. Until then, please tell me a little about yourself and your family."

Michael started telling Officer Dan his story, how he graduated from college with an MBA, married Abby, and immediately began starting a family. They had three children as he climbed the corporate ladder on a fast track to the top rung. Along the way, work consumed his life and to pacify and justify how much he worked; he bought a beautiful home in an upscale neighborhood for his family.

Abby came from a different background and didn't want nor expect a considerable house. She soon fell into the lifestyle of a mom with three kids, trying to lose some of the weight she gained from the three pregnancies, going to the gym when possible, taking the kids to every activity she saw on social media, while begging Michael to spend at least a few hours per week with them.

The entire time, Officer Dan listened and said nothing shaking his head a few times to acknowledge Michael's statements. He only interrupted Michael when the server brought the pies.

"I thought I was living my dream," Michael concluded. "When I was in high school and finishing my MBA, all I could dream about was climbing the corporate ladder and moving into an executive position one day. I loved the power and satisfaction it provided as I climbed, plus the extra money from salary increases and bonuses made me as giddy as a teen with their first dollar earned. I bragged to many of my college buddies how I was making it while many of them were still in an entry level job or a few were struggling while building their own business."

After hearing himself, he put his head down in shame. "I wonder if the dream was to have success or prove to the others that I could do it and show them up along the way. I wasn't the best student in high school. Many kids teased me telling any girl I attempted to date that they would have to work all of their life to pay for my sorry 'butt' and I wouldn't do any better than a minimum wage worker at the local big box store."

Lifting his head, Michael continued. "It wasn't until I went to Junior College that school clicked for me and I sailed through six years of college with a near perfect score,

CHAPTER THREE

never missing a class until the last semester and would have been top when . . ." Michael's voice trailed off.

Officer Dan asked. "What happened?"

"My mom got ill and died before I finished school. I couldn't focus, and my previous grades carried me to graduation. After graduation, I landed a job at a great marketing firm spending a few years there. Then I went to two other firms, each time moving up the ladder, making more money and going further into debt trying to impress people I didn't know."

Michael continued, "My dad was never the same after mom passed, and I tried to talk to him about what I was doing, but each visit, we became more and more distant. Then I received a call from Abby one evening while I was working late, telling me the neighbors found my dad face down in the driveway. He had a heart attack and was there for many hours before someone found him. Maybe along the way, all I wanted to do was prove that I wasn't a loser and would amount to something making my parents proud and shutting up all of the naysayers where I grew up."

CHAPTER FOUR

After a few more minutes, Officer Dan responded, "Michael, you expressed what a dream was, and you put forth the dedication needed to achieve the desire on your heart at one time. If you continued in this direction and remained devoted to this dream, twenty to thirty years from now, will you be at the desired destination or find you climbed a ladder and ran a race that didn't put you where you want to be?"

Before Michael could respond, Nana appeared out of nowhere and slid into the booth next to Officer Dan moving him over, taking Michael's hands into her wrinkled, but soft and gentle hands.

"I was on my way to your table when I overheard what my son asked. Before you respond, can we pray together? My late husband always said that God would give us the desires of our heart as He promised, but we need to ask for desires pleasing to Him and seek the direction that will change our world for the better."

Feeling uncomfortable and not sure how to respond, Michael said, "Um, yea, sure, yea, I guess."

Bowing her head and with Michael's hands held firmly in her hands, Nana prayed for wisdom, guidance, and for The Lord to direct Michael's path.

Releasing Michael's hands, she looked into his eyes and said, "One day, you will be in your sixties, and you will want to go back in time to this day and tell the younger you what you learned over your journey of life. However, that is impossible to go back in time, but my son will take you to visit a few folks in this town who will make you laugh, cry,

CHAPTER FOUR

and gain some clarity. I hope that your heart is open to at least listen to them.

"Young man, I am not sure if you know this, but you ending up in this town wasn't by chance. You are not the first person to enter this diner that needed someone to listen to them or to receive some wise counsel. Look around the diner, filled with people from all walks of life, and over the decades, it has become a haven for many. People can laugh, cry, and seek wisdom because we don't judge. This diner is like an emergency room; we do our best to give you the best emotional attention and life guidance possible. People come to this diner from all over, even after moving away. The goal my husband and I had when we opened this diner many years ago was to create a safe environment for folks that had nowhere to turn when they felt turned off by many mainstream groups. It was to be a place where they were free to laugh and cry without feeling judged. None of us are perfect, nor do we have all of the answers. We want you to feel safe, but most importantly, we pray that you find the courage to at least walk a few steps in this journey called life knowing there are people here to walk alongside you and steady your arm if you stumble along the way. Life is tough, but you need not walk it alone."

It was then that Michael noticed a small plaque cut into the booth's top. "Two are better than one in the journey called life."

"Two are better than one, don't do this thing called life alone!"

As quickly as Nana arrived at the table, she was gone. Michael looked at Officer Dan and asked, "How old is she? The reason I ask is she has more energy and zeal than most people I know my age."

Laughing, Dan responded, "She is in her 80's and has zipped around this diner for as long as I can remember. I asked her one time how and why she moved as she did and her response, 'I am doing what I was called to do and work isn't work and play isn't play, but both are the same to me. One day I will go home to be with The LORD, and my main hope is I was a faithful servant doing what He called me to do, positively impacting many lives along my journey called life.'"

"Michael, explain to me more how you ended up here. What I mean is, what happened that caused you to drive away from your family and sleep in your car?"

After a long pause, Michael responded, "It has been a bad week. If I am open, it has been a bad six months or more between Abby and me. Abby, my wife, and I have been fighting about how much I work, money—money, and how much I work. The fights are always the same, but lately, they became more frequent. I tell her I need to work because we have bills and debt. Plus, this lifestyle. I mean—we fought before, but not like we did this past week."

Officer Dan listened intently, never taking his eyes off Michael as he continued. "It seemed like every hour she would call me at work asking when I was coming home. The kids missed me, things kept breaking around the house that needed to be fixed, and on and on Abby would go. I think she called me ten times at work yesterday, and the last time it was late. I didn't answer my mobile phone, so she called my office. I was so mad that I hung up on her and kept pounding the phone on the desk until it splintered.

"Maybe it was me that cracked first but the phone split in two sending slivers of plastic over my desk. It was a long week, we have a lot going on at work, and I have been going in early. Leaving before the birds wake up and getting home after dark. On Tuesday, I got a room near the office so I could shower then went back to work. I've been working seven days a week for two months, maybe three. My boss is non-stop on me at work and with Abby at me always at home—I was exhausted yesterday. The pressure at work

CHAPTER FOUR

caused me to say things I didn't mean. It wasn't five minutes before Abby called that my boss had chewed me out. I'm not making excuses, but—I guess I am. My boss doesn't know when to stop working and demands us to do and act the same as him. Revenue isn't what it should be and—well, work has been tough.

"When I got home last night, as soon as I opened the door, she started in again. It was about something I can't even remember now. Then she screamed that I never eat her food hot and asking why she even bothers to cook. I don't remember what I said, but as soon as she started about the food, I slammed the door and got in my vehicle and started driving. I shouldn't tell you, but I know I was driving too fast. I kept pounding the steering wheel, and after an hour of mindless driving, I started to slow down when I felt myself dozing off. The rush subsided, and I figured I needed to do something smart and find a place to sleep. I pulled off at the exit and thought that I would take a quick nap. I figured I could find a hotel to stay at for a day or so until I could sort out some stuff. The next thing I remember was you rapping on my window."

Officer Dan responded, "You did a wise thing stopping and resting. As my mom said, you ending up here wasn't an accident. I have a good buddy that you should meet. His name is Lamar. The two of you have a few things in common..."

Cutting Officer Dan off, Michael said, "I don't know—I'm not into sharing and counseling. I think I should go. I mean, no offense, but I've already told you more than I told anyone else—I think ever."

Officer Dan took a bite of his pie and didn't respond, waiting for Michael to continue, but when he didn't, he continued, "I understand. Lamar isn't talkative, but I think you will enjoy meeting him. He has done well in business and has a fascinating place. You can leave your car parked in the diner's lot, I know the police chief, and you won't get towed."

Michael looked to his new friend who had a big grin on his face. Michael remembered he didn't offer to pay for their meal and felt bad about not giving a tip. As he was ready to mention to Dan about the check, he saw Officer Dan hand the server enough money to cover multiple meals with a sizable tip.

"Okay – okay, I will talk to him. You give me your word that this isn't a counseling session," Michael said.

"You have my word," Officer Dan said as he reached out and shook Michael's hand.

CHAPTER FIVE

As they entered the parking lot, Officer Dan pointed to a large white 4x4 truck trimmed out in black. "That one is mine."

Sliding into the truck, Michael noticed it was spotless. He thought about his vehicle filled with crushed coffee cups, bags of half-eaten fast food, and enough crumbs on the driver's seat to feed a family for days.

Within a few minutes, they arrived at a contemporary home set back a few hundred feet from the road. Pulling into the driveway, Officer Dan said, "I will introduce you to Lamar and give you some time alone. I have a few errands to run for my wife then will swing by when you are finished here. Lamar will text me when you are done chatting."

After a quick introduction, Michael was standing alone next to a rugged, but handsome man in his late fifties, who looked like a college athlete that kept up his workout routine.

Lamar warmly greeted him. "Dan sent me a text earlier stated you were coming by and asked if I could give you a little history lesson from my life. If you don't mind, I have a few things to finish in my shop, and we will chat there."

Michael responded, "That's fine." He looked around as he took in one of the most mesmerizing homes he ever visited. It was a modest size home compared to its initial appearance from the outside. He judged it to be between 1200 to 1500 square feet with zero wasted space, and it looked like it could be featured on the cover of one of those contemporary home design magazines. Everything was in order with nothing strewn all over, which was unlike Michael's office and vehicle.

Rather than lingering odors, the home was filled with a pleasing aromatic mix of lemon and orange. Off the back door was a pea gravel path that led to Lamar's workshop. The trail was orderly and lined with green and red shrubs and was void of the usual mix of weeds and overgrown grass.

Walking the few hundred feet to Lamar's workshop, they exchanged general small talk, but Lamar didn't seem as talkative as Officer Dan nor Nana. He appeared reserved and hesitant about their impending chat.

"You know that almost everyone in this town loves Dan and Nana, correct?" said Lamar.

Not sure how to respond, Michael nodded in agreement.

Lamar continued, "A few years ago I was desperate and at one of the lowest points in my life. On a whim, after seeing an ad in a real estate magazine displaying some of the nicest properties near the interstate, I ended up in Nana's diner. She gave me directions to this land, and I fell in love with it. I immediately purchased it and hired an architect and builder to design and build this home long before I realized I would move here. My original thought was to build the home and visit a few times a month as a getaway from the daily grind."

Michael interrupted. "Are you wealthy?" He felt his face flush after he realized how blunt the statement must have sounded. He suddenly felt energy swell up inside because deep down, he wanted to build another home in the country for a place to get away himself.

Lamar chuckled. "I guess it depends on what you call wealthy. When I was much younger than you, I inherited nearly $100k from my parents after they died in a car accident. I didn't want to waste it, so I dedicated my life into building a manufacturing business that grew to employ thousands while stimulating growth to support vendors

CHAPTER FIVE

and other companies in our community. However, while increasing the company's bottom line, I lost touch with my wife to the point I pushed her away. One day, late in the evening, she arrived at my office screaming and accused me of having an affair with my assistant who left hours before. Yes, I had a relationship, but it wasn't with a woman, it was with my work. Unfortunately, my inability to feel any emotion toward my wife drove her to the arms of another man who loved her in a way I wasn't willing to love another human.

As Lamar talked, Michael felt his face flush with guilt, letting out an uncontrolled groan, realizing Abby could feel the same way about his relationship with his work.

"My business continued to grow, and my devotion to the people, and the project seared deep inside me. My dream was to build a plant that would provide for thousands, create extra work for the community, and allow me to give as no one else could. After twenty years of substantial growth, I was wearing out and thought the dream I felt on my heart years ago was wrong. It was on the day when I opened up the real estate magazine I mentioned earlier and saw the ad for this area.

"I dedicated everything to it, keeping the original direction of the company moving while taking care of the employees and doing everything possible to please the customers and community we served.

"Before returning to my office, I stopped at the diner to thank Nana for the directions and my plan to purchase the property and grab a quick sandwich for the road. She suggested I have a meal 'on the house' and sit in the booth at the back of the diner. I am guessing that is where you and Officer Dan sat for your chat. I argued with her for a few seconds concerning the 'on the house' meal, stating I had plenty of money and wasn't a vagrant. However, within seconds, I knew my argument was futile.

"Nana's husband John was still alive at the time, and he slid into the booth a few minutes after I sat down. At first, I was annoyed, not knowing who he was, but after a quick introduction, he said he wanted to welcome me to their town and asked how he could help, sensing something was wrong. We chatted a bit, nothing profound, and when he got up to leave he shook my hand and said, 'the next time you visit, talk to my son.'

Lamar paused for a minute looking out a nearby window reflecting on the memory.

"Little did I know that would be the last time I would see him. He died before my next visit as he attempted to rescue a young girl from a burning building. John was driving home from work as an engineer on a train and saw a building on fire and stopped to help. From the account given by witnesses, John arrived and heard screams of help coming from inside the multi-story home and said he couldn't wait until the fire department arrived.

As Lamar continued, Michael shook his head, and his eyes were wide open in amazement.

"Bystanders stated he ran into the blazing house wrapped in a wet blanket hoping to rescue the family. Within ten minutes of him going in the fire department arrived, but everyone but the young girl died from fire-related injuries. John was found draped over the girl protecting her from the ceiling and beams that collapsed on them. The autopsy revealed his body absorbed all of the punishment as he died from internal bleeding. His body and the blanket kept the girl alive until the firefighters could rescue her. She suffered a leg injury that causes a slight limp, even to this day, but other than that she is doing well."

"What! I, I, I don't understand how she does it," Michael said.

"Who?" Lamar asked.

CHAPTER FIVE

"Nana. How was she able to go on when her husband died such a tragic and sudden death? It seems all wrong," Michael said as he shook his head. "I mean, it seems they—ah, at least she is so dedicated to her God, yet that happened? I don't understand how she could continue serving in such a joyful manner?"

"I am not sure exactly how she does it," Lamar said, "but I heard her respond to a similar question. She said, 'There are times when we don't understand life. John laid down his life willingly for Zoe, and my heart is sad he is gone, but I know I will see him one day again. Plus, there is no doubt in my mind that Zoe will do many great acts in life because of what John did in his life for others and her.'"

"Wow!" Michael muttered. "I don't know if I could ever have that much trust and faith in God."

"I understand," Lamar said. "After the accident, a few things took place in my life, and one of them was I sold my plant to the executive board. They continued the work I began years ago as a small dream in my heart. I used the money from the sale and took a few months off to think then decided to come here and continue with what I love, rebuilding things that others gave up on. I began repairing a few old electric golf carts buying them at auctions around the country, modifying them, and selling to the many senior citizen communities. The work took off because the customers love what I do since they don't look like a normal golf cart."

It was then that Lamar lifted a large garage door to the pole barn they were standing in front of to reveal carts that looked like something you see in an amusement park. Some looked like muscle cars from the sixties, others like the original Model T, with a few that appeared as if they came from another galaxy.

"Are these all yours? I mean, are they all sold?" blurted Michael.

"Yes, I have buyers for every cart you see. Each one is built to spec for the community they will serve. I have a waiting list that goes on for months, and before you say that I should expand the business. I don't want it to grow more than what I have now. I can rescue abandoned carts, serve the senior generation, and provide some work for the guys who pick them up in enclosed trailers to deliver around the country. I do what I can to repurpose parts from many abandoned items."

As Michael stood with his mouth wide open, his mind transported him to his teen years and the hours and days that he spent with his dad rebuilding discarded vehicles, then selling at a fair price with a nice margin. They spent many Saturday mornings scrounging through wrecked cars at a junkyard owned by his dad's buddy from high school looking for the 'perfect' vehicle to save from the 'beast'. Michael shuddered remembering the first time he saw the car crusher that they referred to as "the beast" take a car and flatten it to a mere shadow of its former self and the pain he felt when thinking of any vehicle that wasn't spared the wrath of the beast.

One such Saturday from his teen years stood in his mind. It was the day that his dad said they would pick out the car that would be his when he turned sixteen. They climbed over piles of vehicle wreckage when the perfect 'two' jumped out at them. With the money he saved from working as a caddy at the local golf club and a matching donation from his dad, they selected two Chevy Camaros to build into one Z28 utilizing the best parts from each. Working day and night on the vehicle, Michael ate, drank, and thought of nothing other than rebuilding his new car. His dad's workbench was meticulous, and everything had a place and was in its place. As a teen, he always believed that he would continue what he and his dad did as father and son projects.

CHAPTER FIVE

He recalled his father saying, "Michael, at the end of the day, take time and clean each tool that you use and put it neatly away. A neat workspace . . ."

Michael was brought back to the present when Lamar asked, "Would you like to look at them closer?"

"Yes!" Michael shouted with the energy he hadn't felt in years as he ran over to one modified to look like a '68 Camaro Z28. He slowly slid his fingers along the Z28, tracing each part of the emblem remembering the day when he and his dad put the final coat of paint on the vehicle that would be his. To him, it wasn't work, but a labor of love.

He subconsciously reached into his wallet, pulling out the picture his mom took of him and his dad as they stood next to his favorite vehicle. He inhaled, taking in the smell of new leather and paint and felt a tear fall from his cheek. His fingers continued over the faux leather and to a console that didn't match a '68 Z28, but resembled something from a modern luxury car with a large panel display sporting a broad view from a backup camera and a place for a smartphone and other tech gear.

Looking around the building filled with well-organized shelves, tools, and parts, Michael finished his dad's favorite line when he often quoted Benjamin Franklin, "A place for everything and everything in its place." His father always added, "If you are organized, you will not rebuy things you already own."

Lamar continued. "Michael, although this looks like a classic Z28, there are settings to eliminate the possibility of racing even if the senior citizens wanted to relive their teen years. I have a few slightly larger models that seat four comfortably or transport groceries or similar items."

As a warm breeze moved through the open doors, Michael closed his eyes remembering the late summer nights he spent with his dad working as they listened to the baseball announcer shout on his dad's crackling AM radio.

Crack! As the baseball comes off the bat and the announcer screams "Going, going, gone. Homerun!"

"What do you do?" Lamar asked.

"Me?" Michael stammered. "I am a VP of a marketing firm. Why?"

"Just curious. Do you ever feel you don't live up to or don't belong in that position?"

"Why do you ask?" Michael snapped at Lamar. "We just met, and the question seems a little forward."

"When I was running my company, there were days I would look in the mirror and felt as if I were an imposter. Some will say it is the imposter syndrome while others have other names for the self-doubt. I did some study on the subject since there were days it would consume me. I read where top athletes and executives suffer from this too, and often it is based on high expectations and a feeling like you must be a superhero. The one study I read indicated it was something only women suffered from, but later more studies outlined that it impacts men and women. I often felt like I was lucky, and a quick twist of fate would cause me to be penniless and without a home. Do you ever feel you are in the wrong job or someone will find out that you shouldn't be in your job?"

"Yea, in the company that I work for, we have reports for everything, and there is a daily report that shows the previous day's results. There is a running joke where we all laugh stating we are only as good as today's report." Michael relaxed a bit. "We could have had a great year or even a five-year run, but if the daily report is terrible, we need to have an answer for it immediately."

Michael paused for a moment. "There are many days when I look in the mirror and think, why am I in this job, am I a fraud? How did I get here? I am not better than others. Why do I do what I do?"

CHAPTER FIVE

Lamar said, "I don't have a complete answer, and the main reason I bring this up is because there will be days in your journey called life where you will feel like a failure to your company, your family, and to yourself. I had to look in the mirror and be an encouragement to myself and do everything possible not to retreat into a cave and go into the fetal position.

"One day, as my career peaked and business was booming, I was walking the warehouse floor, and one of my best employees saw me and said, 'Boss, you look down. Is everything okay?' At first, I was startled, here I am the owner, and he didn't have any reservations about checking on my well-being. He asked it in a caring and heartfelt tone. I responded that things were hectic, and at times, I needed encouragement. And when you are the boss, not too many are around to be the encourager. He responded, 'Boss, there was a great king that anytime he felt discouraged would encourage himself in the LORD his God. I am not sure where you are spiritually and don't want to be religious with you, but if a king who was on top of his game needed encouragement, don't get down on yourself if you need to encourage yourself in the Lord.'

"He never went into the subject in any more detail, and I didn't press the spirituality side of it. Looking back, I wish I had asked him more about what he meant, and since living here, I am learning what he implied. However, it made a significant impact on me, and every day after that I would look in the mirror and tell the guy standing there, believe in yourself, don't quit on life or others!

"I am not sure if you are like this or not, but I tend to

"Believe in yourself, don't quit on life or others!"

go solo and do most things myself. It isn't always a good trait nor habit to keep up, but for me, it causes me to impose self-doubt, which creates a feeling of impossibility. Be a friend to others and let them be a friend to you. We might have more things in common than not. As an executive, I knew it was my responsibility to believe in myself. Maybe you feel the same way too."

"Yea, there are days when I feel like—an imposter and believe I let Abby, my wife down. My kids, my co-workers. I heard this once, not only is it lonely at the top but the higher you get, the closer you get to the door," Michael said.

"That's a good saying. I think I need to find someone to make me a plaque to put over my mirror." Lamar smiled.

"Michael, I don't mean to be discourteous, but I hear the driver coming up the driveway to pick up a few carts. I need to help him, but before you go, I want you to leave with a final thought. I learned from my life's experience that dreams change and my earlier idea was to serve the local community by providing work to many families while building a large manufacturing plant. I also had a powerful goal to be wealthy, which fed my ego and pride.

"However, dreams change, but my desire to serve others hasn't and the drive to produce only for the sake of money diminished. I help keep these machines from being scrapped, provide a service while having fun and loving my work to a point where I don't know if I am working or playing.

"To answer your earlier question, yes, I am rich, but not only in the manner you think but in knowing that I help others and have a strong network of friends in this community that will help me and will walk with me on my life's journey. Be safe, my friend, and enjoy life's journey! I am serious, please come back. I would enjoy getting to know you more and bring your wife and children. Although I never had children, I enjoy showing them my toys—I mean, these modified golf carts."

With the last statement, he reached into a small fridge and pulled out a metal bottle filled with water and tossed it to Michael.

CHAPTER FIVE

"Dan is waiting for you at the end of the driveway and will take you to meet Sensei."

Nearly getting hit in the face with the water bottle from a lack of any athletic skills, Michael caught it as it bounced off his shoulder. He floating on air down the driveway with a renewed energy and zeal as he waved to the tractor-trailer driver who was backing up to Lamar's pole barn.

CHAPTER SIX

When Michael reached the bottom of Lamar's driveway, he saw Officer Dan's truck and waved. Jumping in, Michael said, "How was your errand run?"

"It went well," Officer Dan said. "We will stop by my place before I introduce you to Sensei, and we can eat lunch if you are hungry."

"Great! I am a little hungry, but I am not sure why, since I had a great breakfast. Maybe it was the run I just did," Michael responded with an unusual attempt at humor.

Officer Dan looked at him with a puzzled look and said, "Perfect, it is a ten-minute drive on these old country roads. How was your visit with Lamar?"

"I am so sorry about your dad," Michael blurted. "Lamar told me how he died! Man, he died a hero. But I don't understand the faith you and your mom have in your God." Michael quickly looked away out his side window, concerned he had offended Dan.

Why do I just blurt things out, I must learn to control my tongue. For a brief moment, Michael contemplated banging his head against the side window in disgust with himself.

"Yes, dad is a hero," Officer Dan said, ignoring Michael's bluntness and the statement concerning their faith.

They continued in silence until they pulled into the driveway of Officer Dan's home. Reaching up to a button on the visor and pushing it a large gate swung open. As they drove through the gate, Michael looked out in awe of the landscape in front of them. It revealed a nearly perfect manicured property with rolling hills lined with trees and

CHAPTER SIX

ponds sitting at the base of the hills glistening in the sun. He heard the sounds of horses and other animals. Three dogs were barking as they ran down the driveway toward the truck. Dan stopped the truck and scooped up two of the smaller dogs and put them in the backseat of the dual cab truck. They barked and jumped in delight seeing their owner, nearly knocking Michael out of the truck as they attempted to climb into the front seat.

"Boys! Be nice to our new friend. He doesn't know you, and maybe he doesn't care to be bathed with your tongues."

As officer Dan pulled into the small parking area in front of a modestly sized farmhouse with an inviting wrap around covered porch, Michael's mind raced. His heart filled with envy, but he couldn't understand why.

"Michael, this is our home. Come inside, and I will introduce you to my wife and daughter." However, before they were on the porch, the front door swung open, and a teenage girl with the most beautiful colored ebony skin came out.

"Daddy! You are home!" she said as she ran with a slight limp toward Dan jumping into his arms.

He hugged and swung her around holding her tight, then gently put the much smaller girl down. Turning toward Michael, Dan said, "This is Zoe, our daughter."

Upon hearing this, Michael nearly ran into the railing on the porch as he looked back at them, realizing this is the Zoe that Lamar mentioned when describing the young girl that Dan's father protected in the fire. Feeling dizzy, Michael sat on the porch steps putting his hands on the railing in an attempt to steady himself.

"Are you ok? What is wrong? Zoe, please get mom and bring some of her extra sweet lemonade along with a few wet towels. I think Michael is going to need some lemonade to drink while we chat on the swing."

Helping Michael up and to the swing, Dan quietly said, "I guess you put a few pieces of our puzzle together?"

"I don't get it? I don't understand your family? I mean, your dad dies while saving a young girl. Your mom isn't bitter and continues to bounce around like a rabbit, and—is she your daughter?" Michael's voice elevated in volume.

"How . . ." Michael stammered then stopped as he saw Zoe and Dan's wife standing in the doorway, realizing they overheard his blunt statements.

"I - I - I am so sorry, I am so confused. First, you feed me, your mom greets me as if I am an old friend, you take me to visit Lamar, and I learn of your dad's death while saving a young girl. I mean Zoe, ugh! Then I learn that she is your daughter, but she doesn't look like either of you. I - I - I." Michael felt his cheeks turn multiple shades of red, and his ears grow hotter and hotter as he spoke.

Zoe walked toward Michael and took his hands into hers while looking into his eyes. "Mr. Michael, my natural parents, died in the fire when Officer Dan's dad saved me from dying. Mom and Dad adopted me and took me in as their daughter. Their kindness and gentleness with no bitterness toward me are not explainable with words. It can only be explained in the heart as their love pours out on me and anyone they meet. You have only experienced a small portion of their love and kindness. Grandpa John gave his life so I could live, and his love toward me continues through Nana, Dad, Mom, and all of my adopted brothers and other family members. Please drink some lemonade and come inside to enjoy a sandwich with us. We will try to explain."

CHAPTER SEVEN

Upon arriving at the gym, Abby saw Stella, who looked as stunning as ever as the sun glistened off her sweat covered face and body. "How do you do it? You could play the part of any female superhero in a Hollywood action movie." Abby gave her friend a quick hug and marveled at her never-ending energy that matched her loud voice and strong opinions.

"You must check out the new machine they installed upstairs! It is perfect for burning off any frustration and extra energy," Stella shouted over the pounding of loud, energetic music from speakers positioned throughout the entrance of the gym.

Abby thought, *why is all of the best exercise equipment on the second floor? It is too much like work to climb the steps. They really should put in an elevator!*

"Girl, you look like you need a full body massage with the new masseur when we are done working out. He will push all of the knots and frustration out of your body!" Stella laughed as she grabbed Abby's arm and pulled her toward the steps.

Abby wasn't listening as she looked at the steps she needed to climb to get to the new exercise floor. *Will this count as exercise? I don't understand how this is fun for Stella. After a few hours here, I will need a week to recover. Oh well, I do need to exercise!* Abby felt her heart pounding in her chest almost as fast as the beat of the music.

"Is Michael out of town again? It isn't normal for you to come here on the weekend. Are you sure he is on a business trip?" quipped Stella with a smirk on her face.

Abby turned toward Stella, who stood watching Abby with hands on her hips. Her silhouette looked more superhero like than ever as the light coming through the large windows filtered in.

Still recovering from the climb and out of breath, Abby said, "Yes, he is out of town. No, he isn't on a business trip. We had a fight, and he drove off last night to . . ."

Interrupting, Stella blurted, "No doubt to another woman to ease his 'pain' and loosen his muscles!"

"No, Michael isn't like that! I mean. Yes, we had a horrible fight. He wouldn't cheat." Abby felt dizzy from the climb and the conversation. As she made her way to one of the workout benches to sit, her hands shook, and the room seemed to spin as if she were standing on a merry go round. She pulled out her water bottle, opened the lid, in anticipation of fresh water, then mumbled. "Empty! I need to slow down. When will I take time . . ."

"They all cheat! One way or another. I mean, look at this body and face, yet three men cheated on me! They all look and dream, thinking the next woman will make them happy," Stella said with sass in her voice as she rocked with her hands on her hips side to side in an exaggerated manner.

Abby's cry started slowly; then it got deeper and deeper.

"Girl! Tell me—are you sure that he isn't sleeping around or doesn't have a woman on the side? Is he spending more time away from home than normal? Is he saying that he has to work late?"

Abby looked up and said softly, "Um, yea. He has been going in to work on the weekends and leaving before we are up and doesn't come home until late. After the kids are asleep usually."

"Did he come home every night this week or did he sleep at the office?" Stella made air quotes with her hands emphasizing 'sleep at the office.'

"No, one day this week he said he slept at the office ..."

CHAPTER SEVEN

Cutting her off, Stella said, "Girl! The only thing he is good for is his money. I am telling you, he has a lady friend on the side. Maybe two. When was the last time—"

Abby cut her off—"Michael wouldn't cheat on us. He has a lot going on at work."

"Believe what you want, but I know from experience, they all cheat. It isn't a matter of if, but when and how often. Let him be your sugar daddy. As long as he is paying for you to live in that fancy house with an expensive car. He can do what he wants."

Coming over to Abby, Stella sat next to her, putting her arm around her friend and giving her a playful hug. "I think you need a massage more than ever. We will take the elevator to the top floor, I don't want you to pass out before you meet the new guy, but girl, you might when you see him!" Stella said in a seductive tone.

After undressing and wrapping a towel around herself, Abby felt a profound relief that the person scheduled to give her a body massage was a woman and not a man. The thought of another man touching her even as a masseur sent chills of terror through her body. She never let another man touch her except for a simple handshake, and she avoided even a friendly hug.

Putting her face into the spot on the table, the masseuse immediately started, causing her to go into a deep sleep. A recurrent nightmare unfolded, and Abby was a young girl again.

The sound of a vase exploding into hundreds of pieces as it hit the wall woke young Abby from a sound sleep followed by screams of anger. "How dare you cheat on me! You selfish . . ." shouted Abby's mother. Followed by another loud crash as a china closet was knocked over and its contents smashed to the floor. Shards of glass littered the recently waxed hardwood floor.

"You ask, 'how dare I cheat?' when you know that you have cheated on me many times with every man that ever looks at you with a friendly smile and a large wad of money!" Abby heard her father's deep voice bellow as she buried her head under her pillow to shield her ears from the sounds but to no avail. Abby nearly fell from her bed as the sound of a fist being driven through a kitchen cabinet was followed by the slam of the front door and tires squealing. Stones from the driveway pelted the picture window from her dad's pickup truck sped off as if being chased by the police.

This pattern of screams, accusations, and violence filled Abby's youth as her parents accused the other of betraying their marriage vows after multiple adulterous acts were discovered. One parent having an affair is tough enough for a child, but both sent chills through her body with even the mention of possible betrayal.

Unfortunately, for her and her parents, neither parent stopped with one affair, and after numerous relationships and marriages, Abby bounced from parent to parent during her teen years as she experienced her parents' path to destruction. It was almost as if it was part of their DNA never to be faithful to another person.

It developed into a deep-rooted fear in her heart concerning Michael and all of his traveling. When Stella implied that Michael wasn't on a business trip, but was having an affair, her mind raced to all of those horrific childhood memories.

The night Michael proposed to her, she had hesitated and momentarily didn't accept for fear that this day would arrive. Betrayal, then denial, with the inevitable breakup, followed by the never healing heartache. After three marriages for each parent and an unknown number of affairs, Abby's ability to trust in a marriage relationship was minimal.

CHAPTER SEVEN

She had been married the same amount of years as when her parent's affairs surfaced. The fear and possibility of Stella's statement and accusation against Michael ripped Abby's mind and heart apart.

Could Michael cheat on me? Did Michael cheat on me? If so, why? Was he having an affair for years and wasn't going to meetings? Did he have a relationship with someone he traveled with or met while traveling for work? Was he actually with this woman and did she have a family? Did he have a secret family with her, and that is where he is and planning to leave the kids and me?

Abby's tears were muffled by her face buried deep in the towel and masked under the sounds of trickling water and 'relaxing' music coming from nearby speakers.

CHAPTER EIGHT

Michael steadied himself as he made his way to the kitchen table and sat at the first chair he reached. *What is wrong with me? Am I dreaming? I never met people that loved without a catch. I need a cold towel to wipe my face, and why is the room spinning?*

Entering the kitchen behind Michael, Officer Dan, Zoe, and Dan's wife remained quiet, giving Michael time to collect himself and handed him a damp towel. After a few minutes of silence, Dan's wife pulled out the chair next to Michael and moved it in front of him, reaching her hand out and said. "Hi! My name is Ginnie. Welcome to our home. No doubt your head is spinning as you try to put everything you learned into perspective. We adopted Zoe for more reasons that we can explain right now. Please understand that we love her as if she is our natural born child, and that Grandpa John gave his life to save her makes her life even more valuable to us. There is an old saying; 'There is no greater love than when a person lays down their life for another.' John's love poured through Zoe into all of us."

Quickly standing Ginnie continued, "Enough with all of the gushy stuff, I am hungry for some possum pot pie!"

Michael flashed her a confused look. "Really? I, ah, never had possum pot pie."

They all started laughing. "Neither have any of us, but I needed to lighten the mood." Ginnie walked over to the oven and pulled out two sizeable steaming chicken pot pies filled with gravy, vegetables, and plenty of fried chicken for everyone.

CHAPTER EIGHT

Zoe set the table, and they all began eating. Michael couldn't help repeating the phrase, "This is amazing!"

"Do you have room for dessert or do you want to save it for later tonight when you return?" Ginnie asked as she and Zoe cleaned up the plates while Officer Dan answered a call on his mobile phone.

"I would love to have dessert, but if I keep eating, I don't think I will be able to walk."

Dan walked back into the kitchen. "That was Sensei. He asked if we could visit later this afternoon. A last minute appointment put him behind with his private lessons, and he wants to ensure there is plenty of time to chat. I told him that is fine knowing you need time to digest Ginnie and Zoe's amazing food before you hit the mat with him."

Shocked, Michael said, "What do you mean, 'hit the mat'?" His eyes were the size of teacup saucers with a look of terror in them.

"Don't worry, Sensei will go easy on you. Come with me. I would like to show you around the house and property."

Dan gave Michael a quick tour, and every room was filled with some of the most beautiful photographs he ever saw. They had many quotes, scriptures, and sayings as part of the framed prints.

Michael's eyes fell on an image of a silhouetted person on a vast mountain top with the following quote as part of the frame.

"F-E-A-R has two meanings: 'Forget Everything and Run,' or, 'Face Everything and Rise,'" Zig Ziglar.

"Who took all of these pictures? They are beautiful!"

"Zoe took almost every image you see in the house. A few were taken by her mentor, coach, and our dear friend whom you will meet either today or tomorrow if you stay. The image you are looking at is significant to all of us, and that is why we put that quote under it. Zoe's mentor took the photograph of Zoe after she climbed the mountain. She took it from a nearby peak to show the power of having a dream, deciding not to quit, and daring to be different from the norm.

As you know, Zoe's leg was seriously injured in the fire, causing her to limp. The injury has been quite painful. She was told many times that she would struggle with walking, while running or climbing was out of the question.

"However, Zoe knew in her heart that the only way to beat the fear that rose inside her because of the pain was to dedicate herself to prove it could be conquered. In doing so, she has climbed many mountains over the past few years and the images she captured rival some of the best by well-known published photographers. Zoe has inspired many with her pictures and her dedication to helping others that suffer from similar ailments through her work on social media and travels. Additionally, she makes prints and cards and hand delivers them with inspirational quotes to nursing homes and many businesses locally and in nearby towns. Anytime she learns of a need in a person's life; she sends them a card with words of encouragement."

Michael cut in, "Isn't she still a teen?"

"She is seventeen, but Ginnie or I will take her whenever possible. Part of our agreement is to ensure it doesn't impact church or school activity, and she does need some social life."

"Daddy, you are making me blush with all of the bragging!"

They both turned to see Zoe standing in the doorway with a big grin on her face and camera on her shoulder.

"Honey, you know that it isn't bragging if what I say is the truth and everything I said is the truth," Officer Dan said.

"Is it okay if I go with you when you visit Ebony?" Zoe replied.

"Yes, that would be great. Ebony, whom I mentioned earlier, is Zoe's mentor and a great friend of ours. Not

CHAPTER EIGHT

only has she taught Zoe photography, but she guided her through some tough times as she faced the pain in her heart and body. She kept telling Zoe that having a dream is great, but if she did not dedicate herself to the task at hand, the dream would only be a dream never materializing into anything more. Furthermore, if she never did anything with the dream, it would turn into a recurring nightmare called regret."

Zoe walked over to an image of a beautiful waterfall with the sun peeking over the top. Under it was a small brass plaque which read:

Do what you do and do it well and you will have plenty of competition.

Do what you do and do it better than most, and you will command an audience.

Do what you do and do it better than anyone else and you will have the world at your doorstep.

"Ebony said she heard this once and it stuck in her mind as she built a successful photography business," Zoe said. "But her greatest success isn't photography in of itself. Through it, she has coached and encouraged many people along life's journey, living out the mantra that many of us recite in this part of the woods. 'Two are better than one, don't walk life's journey alone.'"

She turned to face Michael. "I became depressed, angry, and frustrated with life, asking why am I here? Grandpa John saved me from the fire, but my natural parents died, and the limp combined with the pain in my body caused me to keep asking God, what is my purpose? Then dad took me to meet Ebony, and she didn't hold back on her advice. I mean, she told me about people born without legs who went on to do great things and have a productive life and about the soldiers that lost a limb or two in war but are running marathons because they wouldn't quit on life.

"During one of our photography chats," Zoe continued, "she kept saying over and over that I must dare to be different and do something so different that it would cause inspiration in others. Why be a success at doing nothing? If I wanted to change the world, then I needed to understand that normal is only a setting on a dryer and I must go after something bigger than life itself. It was then I decided to dedicate my life to inspiring others to not accept normal as a way of life and to quit feeling sorry for myself."

"I miss my natural parents and think of them daily, but I cannot dwell on that loss or live in the past knowing my adopted parents love me in a way that is impossible to explain. God works through them, and they encourage me daily. In a way that words do no justice."

Zoe handed Michael one of her business cards and on one side was the picture of her on the peak, and the other side had her name and under it this inscription:

"Desire to live a life that impacts others. Decide to do what it takes to achieve your dream, dare to be different, and dedicate yourself to achieving it!"

CHAPTER NINE

"Dad, Ebony sent me a text stating she is on her way to Memorial Park and asked if we could meet her there."

"Definitely! We will be there in fifteen minutes."

Except for the music softly coming from Zoe's earbuds, they drove in silence to meet Ebony. Pulling into Memorial Park, Michael thought, *the last time I was in a cemetery was when my dad died. What an odd place to meet Ebony.*

"There she is!" exclaimed Zoe as she waved to her friend and mentor.

Pulling up next to Ebony's SUV and barely waiting until her dad's truck stopped, Zoe jumped out and gave Ebony a big hug.

"Michael, this is Ebony! I owe all of my success to her!"

Ebony cut in, "No, that isn't the truth. I just gave you the nudge and direction. You did the work, kept the course, and didn't get distracted by other 'opportunities' that came along in your life!"

"You gave me more than a nudge!" Zoe laughed.

"It is my pleasure to meet you!" Michael said as he reached out his hand to shake Ebony's. Taking his hand and pulling him to her, Ebony gave Michael a welcoming hug.

Releasing him from the hug, Ebony said, "I am sure you are wondering why we are meeting at a cemetery."

"In fact, yes, the thought crossed my mind a few times."

"Walk alongside me, and I believe you will soon understand."

"Are they coming with us?" Asked Michael as he pointed to Zoe and her dad.

"No, we need a few minutes of private time."

This is creepy. Why did I agree to meet in a cemetery?

"Do you hear that sound? Do you hear that cry and those whispers?" asked Ebony

Stopping in his tracks, Michael didn't move.

"I hear dogs and birds."

"Be still and listen with your whole body. Let your mind relax and don't force anything."

Either I am going deaf, or she is a kook.

"I am sorry, but all I hear are birds and dogs."

"What I hear are all of the dreams lost, the stories that were never written, ideas never implemented, lost passions, and buried ambitions. The graveyard is the richest soil in every town because many people go to their graves with all of their dreams and ideas buried under the weight of life, self-doubt, a lack of ambition, entitlement, and anything else that sears their heart. The cure for some of the world's worst diseases is buried here. The greatest inventions never made it beyond the lips spoken from the potential inventor. Too often, folks went to their graves with many ideas, but nothing implemented because they lacked direction in their life."

"Michael, can you find your way back to your home without a map or GPS?" Ebony asked.

"I am not sure exactly where I am and to answer your question, no. I have no idea which way to drive to get home."

"Exactly, that is the problem with most people too. They have no idea where they are going, how they got there and get upset when they realize they ended up somewhere they never intended. Too often, a new idea or shiny object causes folks to chase 'the' new opportunity only to understand that the saying, 'Everything that glitters isn't gold.'"

Just then a squirrel ran near them kicking up dried leaves in the grass.

"Have you ever come upon a squirrel when driving?"

CHAPTER NINE

Of course! Clenching his fist, Michael said. "Sure! But what does that have to do with anything?"

"The next time you come upon a squirrel on the road, watch them. They dart from one side to the next then back again, never making a decision on which way to go and unfortunately, their lack of decision making, which is a decision, causes their demise. If they had a family, did they have lunch in their mouth for their children? What other squirrel was impacted by their lack of decision-making skills? The wildest part, the squirrels that come after them don't seem to learn from the mistakes of the dead squirrels on the road."

"Michael, see that man over there on the ladder?" Ebony asked.

"I see something in the distance but cannot see that it is a man on a ladder," Michael said with sarcasm.

Ebony handed Michael her camera that had a telephoto lens attached.

"Look through the lens, touch the focus button here," she said as she put his pointer finger on a red button," and tell me what you see."

Hesitating, Michael lifted the camera to his eyes and looked through it, touching the focus button, which caused the image to become sharp and clear.

"I see a man in white painter pants painting the siding of that home."

"Exactly! Before you touched the focus button, you could not see clearly. Correct? After touching the focus button, the scene was clearer, and you needed me to help you learn to focus. Correct?"

Nodding his head in agreement, Michael responded, "Yes."

"I am sure he is doing a great job painting the house, but what if he put his ladder against the wrong house and painted all day? Would he be successful even though he was productive and did a great job? Would the owner of the house he was paid to paint be happy that the painter had his ladder on the wrong house and did a great job? Would the person who owned the house be happy if they didn't want their house painted or if they wanted it a different color?"

"The answer to all of these questions is no. That is what happens to many people in life. They are productive, their heart is in the 'right place,' and they do things with great intentions only to find they didn't stay on the course they were put on earth to do. They are busy, and in fact, often we hear folks greet each other with the statement, 'Are you keeping busy?' What does being busy have to do with being productive and staying on the life path you know you were called to do?"

From out of nowhere, Michael heard a familiar sound. The soft roar of a muscle car from the sixties and lifting the camera back to his eyes, he searched until he was able to see a cherry red Z28 with black stripes on the hood cruising a nearby street. His smile stretched from ear to ear, followed by a tingling that went up his body, remembering the day he backed his Z28 from his dad's garage.

It was then that Ebony asked the question that hit Michael as if he were kicked by an angry mule.

"Michael, are you discontent with your life? Most will never change for the better until they are in debt, distressed, or discontent with their life!"

I am in debt beyond belief, distressed at work and how it impacts my family, and discontent is an understatement.

"Yes, I am very discontent with my life, but we are in so much debt that I need to keep working at my high-stress, well-paid job and all of this . . ." Michael stopped as he thought of Abby and his children and fought off tears while handing Ebony her camera.

Michael continued, "I am sure that my decisions caused my heartache, but I don't know what to do. All of this sounds good in theory, but how can I change, how can I go after what I love to do?"

CHAPTER NINE

"I can't tell you what to do since you will need to make the decision, but I will leave you with this last thought. There are many people in this town and no doubt in your life who will walk with you providing guidance and help. I am sure you heard this saying, 'two are better than one, you don't need to walk through life alone.'"

"Michael, my heart's desire is that you find direction for your life and understand that you ending up in our wonderful town isn't an accident. Life is made up of choices, and we need to live with them. It was your choice to drive toward this town, stop, and allow folks to give you some guidance. But it is up to you to make a choice and do something with the lessons you learned, ideas provided, and friendships built while you are here."

"It is a choice you need to make to open your heart to change. I cannot make 'the' choice for you just like I couldn't make 'the' choice for Zoe to get out and do something with her life. I would love to chat more, but I need to get moving since it is getting close to what we photographers call the 'golden hour'. The sun is setting over the lake on the west side of town. It is beautiful this time of year, and I would like to get a few images and reflect on the beauty of the sunset. I am meeting a dear friend and colleague, Dr. Frank and a few other photographers for a golden hour and blue hour photo walk."

As they walked back to Officer Dan and Zoe, Michael's mind was racing with what he learned during the day, settling on the uneasy feeling in his gut how he left Abby. He suddenly wondered if she tried to call him, remembering he turned off his phone.

They all exchanged goodbyes, and after closing the door, Michael asked; "Is it okay if we call it a night? I need to find a place to stay, call my wife, and process the day."

Officer Dan responded, "Yes, we can call it a day, and you can stay in one of our cottages on the property. There is a one bedroom place that isn't large and is vacant the next few days before some travelers arrive and you are welcome to use it as a gift from us to you."

"I will pay you for the stay!" Michael blurted, then turned beet red, realizing he almost shouted his response.

"Seriously, it is our gift to you. It is ready for use, but if you want to leave a nice tip for the cleaning person, that is fine."

"Dad! I am the cleaning person," exclaimed Zoe.

Laughing, Officer Dan responded, "Yes, I know honey, but you do a great job!"

"Text your mom and ask her if she can grab one of your brother's running suits along with a basket of fruit and nuts and take them to the vacant cottage."

Twenty minutes later they pulled up to a small log cabin with a wraparound porch and a lit candle in the window. They said their goodbyes and Michael watched as they drove back to the main house. The dust glowed as it kicked off the tires of Officer Dan's truck illuminated by the setting sun.

Opening the door, the soft glow of a fire and the smell of cedar coming from a small wood burner greeted Michael with an illuminated path. Looking around, he noticed the cabin couldn't be much more than six hundred square feet in size. He reached for a light switch but soon realized this cabin was off the grid and the only light was from the candle and fire which quickly took the chill from the air in the cabin.

Removing his shoes, suit coat, dress shirt, and pants, he sat on the end of the bed intending to call Abby. However, the warmth and smell of the cedar in the fire combined with lavender essential oils sitting in a small warmer caused drowsiness to overtake him, and he laid back on the bed to 'study his eyelids' for a few minutes.

The next sounds he heard were birds chirping and the distant sound of an approaching vehicle crunching the gravel as it approached.

CHAPTER TEN

After a fitful night of no sleep, Abby woke with a foul taste in her mouth trying to clear the fog in her head. *Did I do something stupid?* The slight move to toss off the covers caused her head to explode with pain. *What is that awful smell? Oh! It's me! I need a shower and coffee! What is all over my bed? How disgusting!* Abby looked at her bed, and she saw it a tangled mess with remnants of the previous night on one of the pillows.

After the massage, Stella suggested they drive around town for a quick dinner and drinks. They went to a sports bar. A few guys attempted to pick her up and then would get mad when she told them she was married and didn't drink. 'Lady, then you need to wear your wedding band unless you really are looking to get picked up, and you sure are acting as if you have been drinking all night!'"

"I can't wear my ring because—after my third child—my finger and hand breaks out in a rash and swells making it impossible to . . ." She muttered after the third guy yelled at her.

She remembers arriving home tired and frustrated, then called her aunt, who never had children, if she wanted some AU (aunt and uncle time pronounced awe) with Abby's kids. Before the words were out of her mouth, her aunt agreed and arrived an hour later to whisk them away to fun, food, and adventure for the rest of the weekend.

Michael heard a slight tap on the door and quickly looked for his pants and shirt, finding the clothes that Ginnie left for him, he dressed and answered the door.

Standing at the door, wearing a beautiful dress and smile was Zoe.

"Hi!" Then she noticed Michael's outfit.

"I guess dad failed to realize how tall my brother is compared to you."

Michael looked down and laughed with her as he realized her brother must be at least three inches taller than him.

"We are going to church this morning. You are welcome to come with us, but if not, that is fine. My parents said you could use the main bathroom for a shower if you don't want a solar heated version in this cabin. The water doesn't get real hot this time of the year out here, and the main house has a regular water heater. There will be food on the stove if you are hungry and my mom said she would leave the coffee warmer on too."

"Thank you!"

Wow, these folks open their home and let me do what I want. Of course, they are active in the church. I wouldn't be surprised if they were the mayor and judge too.

"I will take you up on your offer for church another day. I need a shower and some stiff coffee to wake up, plus I still need to call my wife."

"Great! We will be home around thirteen hundred," Zoe said as she hustled to a modified golf cart.

Is that golf cart a camera? Thirteen hundred?

Seeing Michael's puzzled look, Zoe said, "Oh, I am sorry, my dad spent time in the military, and we always use the twenty-four-hour clock. We will be home at One PM."

Can they read minds too?

After spending the morning bowing to the porcelain throne and her face in a place it should not be, Abby attempted to bury her head under the covers.

Why won't that ringing in my head go away?

She tried to bury her face under one of the pillows to cut the blinding sun as it pierced her eyes.

CHAPTER TEN

I remember ordering a virgin drink with Stella, or did I? Stella, what did we do? Where did we go? What...

Ugh! That stupid ringing!

Then Abby realized it was her phone as she knocked over a bottle of water and aspirin reaching for the phone and fell off the bed when she saw it was Michael.

"Hello! Michael! Are you okay?"

With excitement in his voice, Michael said, "Abby, the folks here are so kind, they have opened their home to me, and I met this woman..."

Upon hearing, 'I met this woman,' Abby ended the call in disgust while tossing the phone against the bed.

Michael continued, "I met this woman whom everyone calls Nana and... Abby?" Thinking they lost the connection, he redialed, but Abby didn't pick-up. After trying a few more times, he noticed a text from Abby.

"Michael, how dare you! Having an affair then sounding so happy about it! You disgusting pig! Stella was right; you are having an affair! I don't want to hear from you!"

Feeling hurt, confused, and angry, Abby blocked Michael's number to avoid him calling her or texting her repeatedly.

Michael attempted to call and text but realized Abby blocked his number. He mumbled to himself, "Good grief, Abby, I wouldn't have another woman in my life. I can't figure out one, let alone two. I love you with all my soul and never would have an affair with another woman! Don't quit on me. Don't give up on us! Who is Stella?"

Michael laid back on the bed in the cottage with all of the life drained from him as he started to cry.

Not knowing what else to do, Abby called the only person in her life that always seemed to provide a solid answer.

"Grandma, do you have some time to chat this afternoon? Great, I will be there as soon as I can, I need to get a shower and—."

Grandma was always there for her, even walking her down the aisle when her parents refused to come to her wedding because they didn't want to see her make the same mistake they made. Grandma wasn't her real grandmother, but a neighbor lady from where she grew up, and everyone called her grandma because she was filled with wisdom and had great cookies too. Grandma was old then. How old is she now? 100? I better get there before she dies!

After getting a shower and putting on some makeup to cover her puffy eyes, Abby drove as if attempting to break the land speed record, crying the entire time.

"Abby! I am so glad to see you!" Grandma said as she opened the door to greet Abby. "Wow! You don't look well, child! You look as if you are trying out for a part in a play as a raccoon! Are Michael and the kids okay? You have makeup all over your face!"

Yep, this is Grandma. As blunt as ever! And why I love her so much!

"No, I think Michael is having an affair! He called earlier, and I hung up on him! He was so excited to tell me about some lady he met and her family."

"How did you get the notion he is having an affair?" Grandma said.

"Well, Stella said that all men cheat and Michael couldn't be going on as many business trips as he says he is."

Grandma kept nodding her head as Abby poured out accusations nonstop for fifteen minutes.

While Abby was talking, Grandma got up and poured them both a cup of tea and brought some cookies.

"Do you want sugar or honey? I don't have any of that artificial sugar stuff."

"Whichever you give me is fine," Abby replied.

Grandma responded, "Hmmm."

With that response, Grandma poured both sugar and honey in Abby's cup, causing Abby to turn and look at

CHAPTER TEN

Grandma with a confused expression. Continuing, Grandma asked, "Would you like one or two cookies?"

Abby said, "Either is fine for me." Another "hmmm" from Grandma followed by breaking one cookie into two, placing them around the teacup stating, "Two are better than one."

Abby's mind was racing, *why was Grandma acting this way? I came here to get some wisdom and a shoulder to cry on, and all I am getting is rude treatment. I am ready to leave.*

Looking up, Abby saw Grandma looking into her eyes with a deep sense of care and compassion.

"No doubt you are wondering why I mixed your sugar and honey and broke the cookie into two," Grandma said. "Honey, two are better than one. You are like the cookie that I broke in two; it needs put back together to be whole again."

"I don't understand."

"Those were simple illustrations, but it is obvious that you need to make a decision. Not deciding is a decision in itself and too often is the byproduct of FEAR . . . Do you know what FEAR means?"

Before Abby could respond, Grandma continued, "I will tell you. It means False Evidence Appearing Real and knowing Michael, you have false evidence."

"There are three sides to every story:

- His side
- Your side
- The truth

You know what they say when we assume?"

Abby said, "Yes, we make an . . ."

Grandma cut her off—"No, when we assume, too often we don't take time to listen and get the facts about what is causing heartache and pain in those we love."

As if on cue, when Grandma got up to take the teacups to the sink, the wall phone rang.

"Hello. Yes, she is here."

"Abby, it is for you."

"Who is it?"

"A lady named Ginnie."

Is this the 'woman' Michael mentioned? How did she find me? How dare she call me here!

Jumping up from her chair so fast, the chair slammed against the wall. Snatching the phone from Grandma, Abby shouted into the phone. "How dare you call me here?"

In a calm tone, Ginnie responded, "Abby? My name is Ginnie, and my husband and I are outside the door, and we would like to come in and talk to you."

"About what?" Snapped Abby to Ginnie in the phone. She was pacing around the kitchen as if on a dog leash as the phone cord wrapped around her body.

"Abby, my name is Officer Dan. Ginnie and I would like to talk to you about Michael."

"Michael, is, is, he okay?" said Abby knocking the nearby chair against the wall as she collapsed on it.

Abby didn't hear the knocking on the door, nor Grandma answering it, letting Ginnie and Officer Dan into her home.

CHAPTER ELEVEN

Michael used the solar heated shower then spied a go bag in the small bathroom closet. Opening it, he found a survival knife, hatchet, bug spray, and a few other items including folded trekking poles. Using the survival knife, he cut the exercise pants to fit, hoping Officer Dan's son wouldn't be upset for ruining the pants. At the bottom of the closet was an old pair of hiking boots that were too large, but he figured they would be better than attempting to walk the woods wearing dress shoes with bottoms slick enough to skate across waxed hardwood floors.

Grabbing the fruit left by Ginnie and adding water to the bottle given to him from Lamar, he noticed it was one of those filtering types he saw on the internet. *Thank you, Lamar, I might need this later.*

Walking out the front door, he paused, turned, and then walked toward the sunrise feeling the fresh morning air on his face. After a thirty minute walk into the woods, climbing over underbrush, fallen trees, and rocks, he heard a low roar. Approaching the sound as it became almost deafening, and the light coming off the water blinded him. He stumbled into a briar bush, and except for a tree branch that his shirt caught on, he would have fallen head first into the base of a waterfall one hundred feet below where he stood.

This place is amazing! Oh, the days that we would hike when not working on cars. Mom and dad would love this place!

Sitting on the edge of a rock, Michael took off the boots to give his feet a rest soaking them in the frigid but soothing water. He drank the water from the bottle and filled it, knowing he would need it for the rest of his journey.

After putting his boots on, he found a small cave that was only ten feet deep and close to six feet high at the entrance and it sloped down in the back of the cave.

Wow! I haven't gone on a hiking trip since—Since I went off to college.

Putting the go bag on the ground and using it as a pillow, he fell into a deep sleep ignoring the dirt and mud he was laying on.

Michael woke when he 'felt' someone or something near him. He heard a voice that was more like a roar because of the effect of the cave.

"Michael!"

Looking up, he saw a man who appeared larger than life. He was dressed in white, backlit, and glowing from the sun coming into the cave. The light glistened off the waterfalls creating an illusion that a giant stood in the cave's opening.

"Michael, my name is Gabriel," said the man as he reached out his hand to help Michael stand.

Filled with fear, Michael stood up, smacked his head on the sloping ceiling of the cave as he scurried back away from the figure. He slipped backward on mud into the back of the cave.

"Michael, I am a friend of Officer Dan. Many call me Sensei."

Placing a small yoga like mat on the ground and from a standing position, he crossed his legs. He sat in an agura style on the mat with his hands on his knees, palm up in the opening of the cave and gestured for Michael to approach.

With his back against the wall, Michael was shaking in fear wishing he had grabbed the hatchet or knife from the sack.

"If you are a friend of Officer Dan, then why are you not at church with him and how did you find me?"

CHAPTER ELEVEN

"Come sit, and we will chat," Gabriel said.

"No! Answer my questions!"

"Okay, first, I am not with Officer Dan for two reasons. The first, I am Jewish, and we worship at the synagogue on a different day than Sunday. Second, Ginnie and Officer Dan went to visit your wife . . ."

"Abby? Is she okay? How did they find her?"

"First, I am sure she is fine. Second, have you heard of the internet and search engines?"

"Yes! I heard of the internet! But that doesn't explain how you found me!" Michael shouted in an attempt to be heard over the waterfall as anger welled up in his body.

"Please come toward me and sit. I will not hurt you. If I wanted to hurt you, I would have done so earlier as you stumbled through the woods and nearly fell into the waterfall earlier."

"You were stalking me?"

"No, I have been watching you since you arrived, waiting for this moment and determining if you would be ready for me."

"Watching me?"

"Yes, do you remember the server in the diner dressed in white? Do you remember the truck driver at Lamar's with the white ball cap and shirt? How about the gardener dressed in white in the cemetery near the large tombstone and statue?"

Michael closed his eyes, and his mind raced back to those moments, and he remembered the people, but could not remember their features nor anything about them.

"Many people visit our town, and some are in a situation like you, but few are ready or willing to make changes needed in their life, and they've never met me in person."

Michael approached Gabriel with caution and noticed that his visitor was wearing a white pair of pants with a loose fitting white jacket similar to martial arts jackets with no emblem or insignia.

Sitting across from him, Michael reached out his hand and shook Gabriel's hand. It was a firm, but not crushing handshake. His hand was warm, not clammy and wet like Michael's as his body dripped from fear induced sweat.

"Michael, every day, you are presented with many opportunities and choices, but often, we don't take time to seek guidance or help from others. A wise king wrote that there is safety when you seek counsel from others. Is there anyone in your life whom you seek out for advice?"

"Yes—I mean, at work we seek counsel from legal and HR before deciding. We meet as a team and work through ideas and how we should proceed when developing new strategies."

"What about in your personal life? Is it any less important than your work life? I guess that you went to college and when in college you learned from professors and maybe had a study partner or two. Correct?" Gabriel asked.

"There were a few of us that studied together, but when my mom passed—" Michael stopped talking for a few minutes as the pain of his mom's death gripped his body.

"I went off on my own."

"When you went off on your own, did your grades improve or go down? Was college easier or tougher on your own? What about life? Was it any easier?" Gabriel's list of questions made Michael's head spin.

"When my mom passed, my grades went down, but—I, ah—yea, college, and life was tough. I became a recluse for some time."

"Everyone needs others to help in a time of need. One of the greatest leaders of all time needed his brother to hold up his arms when in battle. One of the most influential kings had a best friend, and their friendship was so strong that the king promised to take care of his friend's family for life when his friend died. Michael, if the greatest leaders needed others, don't we all?"

Not knowing what else to say or do, Michael shook his head in agreement.

Reaching into his jacket, Gabriel pulled out a note card and handed it to Michael.

Michael looked at the card then turned it over to see:

| OPPORTUNITYISNOWHERE |

"What do you see?"

"A bunch of letters!" Michael snapped, thinking Gabriel was playing with his emotions.

| OPPORTUNITYISNOWHERE |

"Look again, please," Gabriel said.

"Opportunity is Nowhere."

"I see Opportunity is Nowhere!" Michael said. With an emphasis on 'No'.

Opportunity is now here.

Gabriel repeated. "Now, look again, close one eye to focus."

"What?"

"Look again, close one eye to focus."

Closing his right eye, Michael focused, and he saw words pop off the card.

"I see 'opportunity is now here'," Michael exclaimed. Now seeing the letters differently than the first two times, he again looked at the card.

"Good, look again and tell me with both eyes open if you also see opportunity is nowhere."

"Yes, I see both now, but when I focus, I see opportunity is now here."

"Great, everything in life is a matter of perspective, and our experiences and viewpoints often cause us to interpret life's lessons differently than someone else.

"This illustration is like an optical illusion art or when you see a picture within a picture. Once you see the image within the main image, you can never go back to not seeing it. It is the same thing in life when the truth is revealed to you. You can no longer go on believing a lie and expect it to be the truth.

"Michael, too often us men believe that we don't need others. Too often, we permit life to become unbalanced. It is imperative that you learn from life's experiences and the opportunities presented to connect with others who will help you and guide you through the journey of life."

CHAPTER TWELVE

"How did you find me? Who are you really? What do you want?" Peppering Ginnie and Officer Dan with questions, Abby continued non-stop.

When Abby paused to catch her breath, Officer Dan responded, "Grandma is an internet sensation with nearly one million followers on her social media channels, teaching wisdom and life's lessons through hilarious videos and amazing one-liners."

"Really? I never knew? I mean I watched a few videos when you started, but stopped watching them when I got busy—Grandma, I am sorry I didn't watch more of your videos," Abby said.

"No worries honey. There is an old saying, 'A sage has no honor or wisdom among family and friends.'—It is my paraphrased version," Grandma said as she chuckled at her own sarcasm.

"Zoe, our daughter, did some reverse searches or something, and it wasn't long before she was able to determine your connection. Grandma once posted a video and pictures of you when you lived near here, and earlier this morning she posted a selfie of her making cookies saying you were visiting later today."

"I never knew—wow! Grandma the sage." Abby burst out in tears, followed by laughter.

After fifteen minutes of non-stop questioning, Ginnie and Officer Dan convinced Abby to leave her car at Grandma's and travel with them to meet Michael and the other woman—Nana.

Climbing in the backseat of Ginnie's white SUV with Officer Dan in the driver's seat, Abby noticed a large picnic style cooler.

"In the large cooler like box is Nana's breaded chicken with a container of mashed potatoes baptized in garlic butter, freshly baked bread, and pea-can nut cookies. I am sorry, but it isn't gluten-free. I hope it's okay," Ginnie said.

Reaching down to open the container of food, the aroma filled the vehicle, and she noticed everything was warm as if it just came out of the oven.

Seeing her reaction, Ginnie said, "The cooler is one of those fancy kind that keeps the food warm with some sort of heating element. The other smaller cooler has sodas, iced coffee, and water. But it is a normal one with ice. The iced coffee is a brew Nana came up with many years ago, long before the chain coffee shops started selling it. Her coffee has a nice kick to it. She says it is much better than those sugary energy drinks."

Abby devoured the food as if she hadn't eaten in days and drank two small bottles of the coffee. She was uncommonly silent for the first hour as she ate and listened to some of the most soothing music she ever heard. She interrupted the silence to thank them and state how good the food was, she realized she failed to offer them anything to eat or drink.

After the first hour of silence and the coffee kicked in, Abby asked question after question about them, their family, Nana, their town, and more. Without wanting to reveal too much, they kept saying, "Nana will explain when we meet Michael at the diner."

CHAPTER THIRTEEN

"Hold on, you said Abby is on her way here?" Michael was stunned.

"Yes, Abby is on her way here. I can explain more as we hike to my Jeep. It isn't far from here." Gabriel said.

"You knew I would come here?"

"I figured that you would come here or to the lake where the water eventually stops on this property. My gut said that you would come here. Do you remember the waterfall image at the house?"

"Yes."

"That image is a picture of this waterfall and a favorite place to visit for many reasons, but you don't want to drink the water," Gabriel smirked.

"Really!" Michael gasped.

"Just kiddin'!"

They both laughed and hiked to Gabriel's vehicle making some small talk.

When they reached Gabriel's vehicle, he turned to Michael and said, "Listening to you it seems you have been doing a life of mental and manual labor, but you need Emanuel labor in your life."

Not understanding the meaning, Michael grunted. "Hmmm."

The trip to Nana's place was in silence, and it seemed as if the talkative Gabriel had said what was needed and didn't want to spoil the impending moment when Michael, Abby, and Nana sat down for a 'chat'.

"Wait! I need to get cleaned up, my clothes look atrocious!" Abby screamed when she realized they were not far from their destination.

"We've got you covered and will stop at a friend's place, Ginnie said. "She has a second-hand clothing shop with a place to change and get cleaned up. We have the key and will find you something. We can just leave her the money on the counter."

Officer Dan waited in the SUV while Ginnie and Abby pursued finding a dress and shoes. They were laughing as they searched, and Abby tried on prom like dresses followed by laughter and fun teasing. At one point, Abby came out in a tiara and oversized gown, which made them both fall to the floor, laughing and giggling like two teen girls. They settled on a simple sundress and matching sweater.

"Do you think Michael will think I look pretty?"

"Honey, you look beautiful, and I am sure Michael will fall all over himself when he sees you!"

Abby said. "Thank you. Please let me pay. You have been so kind."

"It is our gift to you. I will lock up and meet you in the SUV."

"Sensei sent me a text stating Michael is at the diner in 'The Booth,'" Officer Dan said.

"'The Booth'?" Abby asked.

"You will soon find out, we are not far from Nana's Place, and Ginnie will take you to the door, but then both of us will leave. Michael's car is at the diner, and we hope to see you later this evening," Officer Dan said.

Michael sat in the back of the diner in the same booth that he sat with Officer Dan the day before, but it seemed like weeks had transpired. Sensei left after informing him that Abby was on her way and would arrive soon. He wouldn't be far and available to help if needed but assured him that Nana would be a better help.

CHAPTER THIRTEEN

Hearing the bell to the front door, Michael looked up and saw Abby standing in the doorway glowing from the sun as it poured into the diner through the open door. The sun illuminated her as if she was a heavenly being. Michael nearly fell out of the booth as he attempted to stand, his legs caught on the table. If it had not been bolted to the floor, it would have flipped over. It was then that Michael saw himself in the mirror behind the counter for the first time after his trek in the woods and realized he looked haggard. He hadn't shaved for a few days, and his hair was a mess looking like a bird's nest. The contrast between the fast approaching Abby and he was like something from the children's movie of a beautiful woman and an ogre.

As Abby approached, out of nowhere, Nana appeared and ushered Abby next to Michael rather than the opposite side, which was where Abby started to sit.

"Are you hungry? Thirsty?" Nana asked, taking total charge of the situation.

Without waiting for an answer, she whisked away and quickly returned with a pot of fresh coffee and two slices of pie.

"I will let you two chat for a few minutes, but I will return, and we will chat." With that, she was off again.

Michael said. "Abby, you look amazing! Wow! I, I, I am so sorry!"

Stumbling over his words, Michael kept saying how beautiful she looked, how sorry he was, and on and on. He babbled as if on a first date with Abby.

Abby attempted to console him while apologizing between breaks in his sentences when Nana slid in across from both of them.

To break the tension, Nana asked, "What stinks?"

Embarrassed, Michael said, "I am sure it is me."

They all laughed, and Nana pulled their hands into hers, looked back and forth at them, and then uttered a simple statement.

"Don't Quit!"

"I can tell you about famous people who faced obstacles, but they don't have the same meaning in my heart as my family and friends that never quit when life got tough!"

CHAPTER FOURTEEN

"Don't Quit!"

"There are times when life seems to deal us a horrible hand and to quit seems more

"Don't Quit!"

natural than going on. Michael, it was no accident that you showed up in our town. Abby, it was no accident that Zoe was able to help my son and Ginnie find you.

"The toughest lessons we learn are those learned from our mistakes, but only if we choose not to repeat them. I am sure that you've been told to never take financial advice from a broke person nor to take weight loss advice from a plump woman like me." Nana laughed at her joke.

"However, you should take advice from people that overcame challenges in life and didn't lie on the ground in a fetal position. Michael, you met Zoe, and Abby, I hope you take the time to meet her too. She overcame severe challenges losing her parents in the fire. That combined with her injury, then being adopted into a new family. She could have quit many times, but didn't.

"One day, you will meet our mayor, who dropped out of school then worked hard to get his G.E.D. when all of his family and friends laughed at him the entire time he struggled and studied. After getting his G.E.D., he went on to get an M.B.A., built a consulting firm, and then retired and came to our town to be mayor. Betty Sue, the town comptroller and math genius, failed math all through school, but when she went to junior college, a professor took her under her wings and helped her discover her love for math that was buried under traditional learning.

"Then there is Gabriel, better known as Sensei. Growing up, he couldn't do anything athletic even if he worked at it day and night. He wasn't accepted into the military, but one day out of desperation answered a small ad in the back of a magazine advertising martial arts instruction. He figured, 'why not' and signed up, quickly learning that his Sensei could teach like no one he ever met, and after hours of practice soon became the school's best student. Rapidly advancing in the ranks, he went on to win many regional and national championships in the style his school practiced. After winning for many years, he grew bored and frustrated with the direction of his life and wanted something new. It was after a major tournament that he won where he met my late husband who was traveling on business. He invited Gabriel to our town to set up a school for wayward boys and girls."

Nana continued, "I can go on and on explaining about the single moms who raised their children after their no-good husbands left for so-called 'greener pastures' or the teachers who took time to educate children and created a love of learning in them that would last a lifetime. There are the men and woman at the shelters that work day and night rescuing children from poverty and horrific situations. These folks face challenges, but they didn't quit!

"Then there are the people who sit by loved ones in their latter days—who never quit on them, helping them through dark hours.

"These are the folks who are not social media heroes, but heroes to their family and friends. You have the parent who works two jobs so their children can have a better life than they did. The people who study day and night searching for the 'cure'. The couples who stayed together even when life got tough and never quit! My husband and I were married for more than fifty-five years when he died from injuries in the fire. We had rough times, and we had great times.

"You met Dan but will never meet our other son, Stan. We lost him due to addiction to pain killers after he suffered a debilitating back injury. We could have quit on each other or life, but we didn't during the challenging parts of life. Early in my husband's career, he met a man who challenged him in a way that no one else ever could. My husband was very kind, but at times was 'challenging' to live with for reasons he couldn't understand. The man told John that he must have a dream for everything in life. What was his dream for his marriage and family? What was his dream for his relationship with God and so on? Too often, folks will have one dream and pursue it failing to have a dream for each aspect of their life. John's dream was to be married for life, and when folks asked how long we were married, he would say 'we are celebrating our fiftieth' causing people to stop in their tracks. Mainly because we were in our thirties at the time."

Nana paused, handing Abby a tissue to wipe tears streaming down her face.

"I wish I could have met him," Michael said.

"Actually, you did," Nana said.

"I did? How? He is dead."

"Not in person, but his impact lives on in others. The man he met became a great friend and mentor, encouraging John to do things that will positively impact others. John told me that everyone makes an impact on the lives of others. Some in a positive way and others in a negative manner.

"Zoe is a result of John's impact as well as Dan and Ginnie. He impacted me, and I impacted him. All of the people in the diner and those we meet are impacted by us. How we respond to a situation impacts the lives of others. When we were helping Stan work through his issues, John stated he was very depressed and wanted to quit 'helping' others because of the emotional drain. Then one day as if sent by God himself, a man approached John in a grocery store and practically knocked John off his feet with a bear hug. 'John! Do you remember me?' John stated he looked at the man, but being in a depressed state of mind, couldn't remember him. 'John, a few years ago, you sat with me and provided me words of hope, encouraging me not to quit. This wonderful lady is my fiancé, we are getting married in a few weeks. Because of you, I am here today, I didn't quit, and I am getting married soon.' The man hugged the woman he was with and kissed her on the cheek.

"John said that he floated around the grocery store with a renewed vigor and hope. It was the emotional boost he needed, and only eternity will show the impact John made while on earth. I never met the man that John mentioned, but maybe he went on to help others by his testimony of hope.

"We are having a town picnic at my son's place this evening, and you are welcome to join us, but if you want to go home, that is fine. The invitation to our town is always open. Please visit soon!"

Nana paused, then said. "Take as much time as you need to at our diner, but more importantly, take time to talk to each other and heal the wounds of life.

"Michael, my husband always said that you could tell a man's priorities where he spent his money and time. Most men will say that their family is the most important, but then spend the majority of their life at work or one of their favorite activities or hobbies. If your family is the most important, will you make them the most important? Don't answer today, but the next time you have some quiet time, please consider my words."

CHAPTER FOURTEEN

Placing a small card on the table, she said. "This is the passcode to the main gate for my son's property along with a map and location of the picnic."

As Nana rose from the booth, she reached over to Abby and Michael, softly touched their hands, then quickly turned toward the kitchen wiping a small tear from her cheek.

CHAPTER FIFTEEN

Initially, Abby and Michael didn't move after Nana left the booth, but waited a few minutes. As if on cue, they each reached for the other's hands—then gripping tight as if to keep the other from leaving. Looking into Abby's eyes, Michael mouthed, "You look beautiful! I love you," then leaned in and gave a soft, delicate kiss on her lips. Letting go of her hands, he cradled her face in his hands and kissed her tears as they flowed down her cheeks, saying over and over again, "I am sorry. Please forgive me."

They held and cried together, not concerned with anyone around them. Without a word, Michael rose from the bench, taking Abby's right hand in his left, and they exited the diner.

Sitting quietly in his vehicle, they said at the same time, "Let's go to the picnic and thank everyone for their kindness."

"I would love to meet Zoe and thank her for her sleuth skills," Abby said.

"Who has the kids?" Michael asked.

"Oh, they are at home by themselves, at ten, eight, and six, they are old enough to take care of themselves, and there is a freezer full of food, and they can use a microwave," Said Abby said.

Michael shook his head in disbelief and said, "Really?"

"No, you nut! Do you really think I would leave the kids alone? Stella stayed with them—just kidding! My aunt and uncle have them, which reminds me I need to text her and let her know we will be delayed. She will be glad to keep

CHAPTER FIFTEEN

them, and since tomorrow is a holiday, the kids don't have school."

Backing out of the parking lot, Michael said he thought he remembered how to get to Officer Dan's place, but sent him a text for directions just in case.

Abby sat in her seat wishing that Michael's vehicle had a bench seat so she could slide next to him, then asked, "How much longer until we arrive at Officer Dan and Ginnie's Place?"

After driving a few minutes in Michael's closed up vehicle, reality hit Abby squarely in the face. Not wanting to impact the 'moment', Abby said, "Michael, I don't intend to sound mean, but you might want to stop at a store and get some clothes, a shaving kit, industrial strength soap, and some men's cologne."

"So what you are really saying is I stink and look like a vagrant?"

The silence was so thick even Michael's smell couldn't cut it.

Then they both burst out laughing, and Michael said, "Okay, oh wise one, use your smartphone and find a place near here that is open today."

Ten minutes later, they were walking hand in hand into a store when Abby's phone vibrated from an incoming text message.

"My aunt is thrilled to keep the kids another day. She said to be good, and if we wanted to stay a week, that would be fine."

"A week?"

"No, I added that," Abby said. "It was good to see your expression."

Michael leaned in to kiss Abby, but was stopped when her hand covered her face as she said, "Remember, you stink!"

"Fine!" Pretending to be hurt, Michael slumped his shoulders and shuffled his feet as they walked toward the men's clothing area of the store, then to the lady's section for a few things for Abby, including a few quick dry items.

Thirty minutes later, with a few bags of clothes, toiletries, and some snacks, they were headed toward Officer Dan's home.

CHAPTER SIXTEEN

Pulling into the driveway, Michael entered the code into the keypad, and the gate swung open. Abby said, "Wow! What a place!"

"Yep, wait until you see the cabin that they said we could use. It is quaint, rustic, and very nice. I have never met a family so kind. It seems as if everything they touch is blessed."

Arriving at the cabin a few minutes later, they heard in the distance what sounded like a band practicing.

"Do you think they have a concert going on at the picnic tonight?" Abby asked.

"I wouldn't be surprised based on everything I saw in the past few days," Michael said.

As Michael stepped out of his vehicle, he stopped dead in his tracks. When they arrived at the cabin, he hadn't noticed it because it was sitting in the shadows off to the side of the cabin. He stood dumbfounded.

Abby asked, "What's wrong?"

"Do you see that?" Michael pointed to the modified golf cart that Lamar customized into a Chevy Z28.

Michael walked over to the cart and read the note on the steering wheel.

"Abby and Michael, enjoy this vehicle while staying here. I noticed how you marveled over it."

The note was signed, Lamar.

Sitting in the driver's seat, Michael put his head in his hands and cried tears of joy, then started laughing. Abby approached quietly and put her right arm around him. She gave him a soft kiss on his left cheek.

"You need to get cleaned up," Abby said. "I think we have a full evening tonight."

Abby arrived at the cabin door first, and upon opening it, she noticed the small table had a basket of fruit, snacks, towels, and other toiletries for their stay.

She shook her head in disbelief and sat on a rocker next to the table.

I cannot understand these people. They don't know us from Billy Bob or Sally Sue but pour out more love in a few days than some folks have given us in a lifetime.

Turning to Michael, Abby said, "Why do you think they are so nice? Do you think they are part of a religious cult? I don't understand. I never experienced this type of kindness. Everyone always wants something. My parents were a perfect example of doing things to get something from it. No short or long term commitment to anything."

Michael knelt in front of Abby and held her hands. "Honey, I don't know why they do what they do. If they are part of a scheme, then they put a lot of effort into this ruse, but I doubt it is a scheme. Whatever the reason they do what they do, I would like to learn more about it. Although I have only been here a short time, I like it and feel safe."

While Michael showered and got ready for the picnic, Abby decided to look through the small cabin. She pulled open a drawer and noticed half of a torn page crumpled up.

The page read:

"You must have a dream for every aspect of your life! Too often, dreams are only for career, sports, or education, but having a vision for each element of life is critical. You must have a dream for your spiritual life, one for your physical, financial, and another for your emotional well-being. If you are in a relationship, you must have a dream for its outcome and decide that your relationships will not follow the 'norm'.

CHAPTER SIXTEEN

"This dream must be so real that you are willing to dedicate time and energy to it, knowing that when you decide to make the changes to achieve the dream, you will be different. Decide that being normal isn't what you want because normal is only a setting on a dryer. Although there is nothing wrong with being normal, people that find success in each aspect of life are not normal. Normal is expecting something without direction and dedication. Normal is expecting a fulfilling life without daring to go above the standard routine, and too often folks quit before they achieve their dream, being distracted by other 'opportunities'."

Abby flipped the page over, but the page was torn below the last line, and there was nothing on the back side except a small handwritten note: 'Two are better than one. Don't do this thing called life alone.' Dr. Frank

As she was placing the page back in the drawer, Michael came out of the small bathroom, and she stood up and without thinking, put the crumbled page in a small pocket in her dress.

Walking over to Michael, she put both hands on his face saying, "So soft and smooth. As a baby's behind." Then she kissed him on his face and lips.

CHAPTER SEVENTEEN

Walking hand and hand to the golf cart, Michael thought, *I don't want this emotion to end. What do I need to do to build on what I feel now for Abby, my family, and our future? What is it about this place and those in the town that makes me want to do something so different than what I have been doing?*

Not realizing he stopped dead in his tracks, Abby looked to him and said, "What's wrong? You have a puzzled look on your face with a big grin."

"Nothing. Actually, everything, but nothing. What I mean is, I don't want this weekend to end, but I know that it will and..."

Michael turned to Abby and gave her a soft kiss then picked her up. He carried her to the modified golf cart. They were laughing like two teens, but he was struggling as he carried her to the cart since he hadn't exercised in years.

Abby said, "Don't hurt yourself and don't drop me! We haven't done this in years!"

Michael smiled, leaning in to kiss her on the forehead. After putting Abby in her seat, Michael went to the driver's side and pulling the map Nana gave him from his shirt pocket, he handed it to Abby and asked, "Which way?"

Laughing, she said, "Me? I guess you don't want us to get there tonight."

"Hmmm, yep—Miss directionally challenged."

Taking the map back from Abby, Michael studied it, then headed in a west facing direction down a path cut in the field. Arriving ten minutes later, they parked next to a

CHAPTER SEVENTEEN

row of ATVs, 4x4 vehicles, and bikes, realizing that people came to this cross country and through the woods.

They started to mingle with the others, making small talk, looking around the crowd for someone they knew. Within a few minutes, they heard their names called and turned to see Officer Dan walking toward them.

"I'm glad that you decided to stay for our picnic. There is plenty of food, and later a local band is going to sing a few songs. Maybe you heard them practicing earlier?"

"Thank you for inviting us! We heard someone practicing. They sounded great," Abby said.

"You never told us much about you? I mean, I learned a few things, but we would like to get to know you better," Michael said.

"There isn't much to tell," responded Officer Dan. "Let's get something to eat, and we can sit and chat. I don't like to focus on me, but would rather help others in their life's journey."

Finding a picnic table, the three of them sat away from others, but not so far removed they still could hear people talking and laughing. Seeing children playing and giggling, Abby felt sad, missing her children. She turned away from Michael so he couldn't see her wipe tears from her eyes while she sent a quick text to her aunt to check on the children.

Officer Dan said, "You know part of my résumé. Currently, I work part-time as a police officer and full-time, helping Nana, plus I keep this property in shape. We have a few short-term rentals that people use for weekend 'escapes' and ten cabins that are long-term rentals. We are not far from the interstate, and people like to live in the country, then travel to the city for work. Other renters work from home, and this is perfect for it. Writers and other creatives love to rent the cabins for inspiration and walk the grounds and will sit by the lake here or by the waterfall on the east side of the property.

"I served in the military years ago and did a stint in the Special Forces, and when I got out, I similarly worked for the government, but missed living in the country and moved back here. This property has been in our family for multiple generations, but it didn't always have the cabins or picnic area. Ginnie and I have two boys, and when we came back here, we built one cabin to rent, then another, and before we knew it, we had a small business, renting them out. Initially, I worked full-time as an officer, but couldn't keep it up and do the other things. After dad died . . ."

Officer Dan paused for a few uncomfortable minutes. "After dad died in the fire, Nana couldn't keep up with the diner, and both boys moved away. One is a software engineer and visits when he can, and the other is . . ." Another long pause.

"Ginnie and I have been married for over forty years. We have been together all of our lives. The funny thing about us, we played together as kids but were not boyfriend and girlfriend until our senior year in high school. Then, as they say, the rest in history. You met Zoe, who brought so much life into our family when we needed it most. She overflows with energy and love!"

"Please tell us about your dad," Abby said as she put her hands on Officer Dan's.

Clearing his throat and after a long pause, he began. "He was a great guy. Tough on us at times, but he always wanted to do right by us and others. He was an engineer. I mean the kind that drives a train. One day on a trip, he met a guy that literally changed the future of our family. I will tell you the whole story one day, but here is the edited version.

"My dad met this guy named Miguel who became a spiritual father to my dad and asked him one question that stopped my dad dead in his tracks. 'Are you leading a life worth remembering?' At first, my dad didn't have a clue what Miguel was asking, but through many conversations

CHAPTER SEVENTEEN

over multiple years, my dad changed and understood that everyone has gifts, talents, and are put on this earth to make a difference. My dad became obsessed with making an impact in the lives of others but never concerned himself with being remembered by name. Instead, he wanted what he did to live on forever. My parents had the diner years before he met Miguel, but it seemed once my dad started putting some of the principles he learned in place at home, my mom took on a new zeal at the diner, and she became known as Nana to most of the folks in the town. They understood that individually they made an impact, but the combined effort of our family turned this small town upside down. Blessings seemed to pour out of the sky to us and . . ."

Officer Dan stopped talking and stood to look toward a lone figure walking up the path toward the picnic. Abby and Michael looked at each other, then to the others realizing this person was known by most of the attendees. Even some of the children stopped playing and stood to watch Officer Dan run toward this person at a breakneck speed.

Looking around, Abby watched Ginnie walking toward the figure in slow, measured steps. When Officer Dan reached the individual, he embraced the much larger person, lifting him off the ground holding the hug for minutes.

With the crowd still watching, Officer Dan put the man down and put his right arm around him, and they walked toward the people. Approaching, Abby saw that the man was disheveled, and his long hair was dirty and matted.

It was apparent that not only did Officer Dan and Ginnie know the man, but most of the crowd knew him too.

Holding Michael tight, Abby watched the threesome with great anticipation.

Michael thought. *Who is this man? Why does he look like a vagrant, and why is everyone watching?*

As if on cue, Officer Dan shouted. "Our son Christopher is home! Band, play a welcome tune, and Zoe, get your brother some food please!"

Ginnie hugs them both and Abby could see her tears running down her cheeks and Christopher's as she kisses him over and over. Then, she gently wiped her tears from his face.

CHAPTER EIGHTEEN

As the band played and folks returned to eating, talking, and playing various picnic games, Abby became engrossed with Ginnie, Officer Dan, and Christopher. She couldn't stop watching them. *Apparently, this is the son that caused Officer Dan to choke up in their earlier conversation.*

Unconsciously, she wandered toward the threesome but said nothing as she watched in amazement.

What is his story? Oh well, I am sure that we will learn more later.

Looking around, she noticed that Michael and a woman were near the lake talking, but couldn't make out her features as they were both silhouetted from the setting sun. She felt jealousy creep through her body like never before.

Wow! Where did that feeling come from? I am sure that it came from my parents and their actions. Michael isn't like them.

"Michael, my name is Betty Sue, the town comptroller," the woman said, reaching to shake Michael's hand. "Nana asked if I could introduce you to my husband. He is the guy playing with all of the kids on the field. There are days I don't think he grew out of being a kid, but that is what saved our marriage."

Turning to her, Michael stopped and started to ask, *what do you mean?* However, he hesitated then decided to ask her husband.

Betty Sue waved to her husband to join them. Betty Sue's husband skipped over to them, holding a young girls hand as they laughed and bounced around until the two of them fell on the ground laughing and playing. Betty Sue rolled her eyes as she smiled at them.

"Michael, this is my playful husband, Robbie. Robbie, this is Michael. Nana asked that you two talk. I will do my best to entertain the world."

"Michael, it is great to meet you," Robbie said as he reached out his hand and shook Michael's hand.

"Please accept my apology for the dirt and sweat. My motto is 'time is short, and I plan to enjoy every minute given to me'. My wife is the more serious one. She plays with numbers and—well, we balance each other."

"That is a nice watch," Robbie said. "Lots of fancy dials."

"Oh—it's a gift my parents gave me years ago and—umm, we used to hike and stuff together. I keep it as a memory. I don't hike and play in the woods like I used to," Michael said.

"Can I buy it from you?" Robbie asked.

"Why would you want to buy it from me?"

"Actually, I'd like to buy time from you," Robbie said. "If I give you two hundred thousand dollars, can you give me two hundred thousand dollars of time?"

"I don't follow you," Michael said. *Where is this guy going with these questions?*

"Obviously, the watch has value to you, but the watch is only a timepiece that indicates a measurement. Many will say that it keeps time, but time is relative, and you cannot keep it. What I am asking, will you sell me time?"

"I still don't follow."

"Let me explain! Some will say that time is money. I completely disagree. Because if I offer you a quarter million dollars, you cannot sell me time. You can sell me something worth two hundred and fifty thousand dollars or give me two hundred and fifty thousand dollars of your work, but you cannot sell me time.

"Years ago, I was given a second chance in life after being hit head-on in a car accident. A driver was playing with

CHAPTER EIGHTEEN

their phone and crossed the center line and hit me head on. I died on the scene, but the first responders and subsequent medical people brought me back to life. The accident and time in the hospital taught me two valuable lessons. The first, life happens fast, and I must live each moment to its fullest.

"Additionally, I cannot purchase time. Once I spend it, unlike money, I cannot go out and earn more time. To me, it is more significant than anything I can purchase. Oh, and before you ask, the other driver was okay. They had a few scratches, and no I don't have any ill feelings toward them because the lessons I learned far exceeded anything I knew up until that time and besides what good would staying mad at them do me or anyone else?

"Yes, I suffered scars on my face, but I tease others and say I got them jumping out of a plane after doing a face plant. You should see the looks I get before saying, 'Just kiddin'. I do my best to get folks to laugh, and there are times when I am told that I act too much like a kid. However, my response is always the same. When was the last time you saw a kid go to work daily, take out the trash, clean-up, and do adult things?"

Michael started to respond but thought better of it as Robbie continued on.

"Michael, time is a great asset. There is an old saying that I heard Lou Holtz say, 'What's Important Now? W.I.N.'. He used to tell his players to say this over and over again to drive home the important point. For me, time isn't a commodity to waste and is always important now. I am not sure what you do in life but the time you spend doing what you do, is it taking time away from the things or people you say are important to you. Most guys will say their family is most important, but unfortunately, most of their time is spent away from them. They work hard providing for their family, and there is nothing wrong with that, but too often, we guys miss the value of time. Just like the driver that was playing with their phone while driving. They were attempting to split their time between two things, and we both learned that isn't possible. I learned that I will focus on what I am doing now and always ask this question to the guy in the mirror. Hopefully, there isn't anyone standing behind me when I ask the question but—the time you are spending, is it time well spent? Knowing that you cannot get the time back, are you a good steward of TIME?"

"Before I do anything in life, I stop and ask myself, is this a great use of my time? There are things I can do at home, but often pay someone to do them since my time is better spent on other activities. We own a few acres of property, and I enjoy maintaining it, but when the time I spend on it interferes with other things of more value, then I must look at either not working on our property or hiring someone to do the work."

"I never thought of time in that perspective," Michael said. I was always taught that time is money and money is time. But you are correct, I cannot purchase a block of time to use later. In my line of work, we sell time to the client in advertising slots, time spent on working marketing campaigns, and 'billable hours'. How do you determine, 'what's important now'?"

"There are times when it seems impossible," Robbie said, "but I look at time this way. If I do this activity will it add value to my life, the life of those around me, especially my family, and most importantly, will this use of time impact my current main goal in life."

"What do you do? I mean, what do you do for a living?" Michael asked.

"Ha, ha! I missed the normal guy introduction. I am an author, speaker, and consultant. I teach and speak on the topic of priority management . . ."

CHAPTER EIGHTEEN

Interrupting, Michael asked. "Priority management? What is that? Is it like time management?"

"Sorta, many teach time management, but my philosophy is that time isn't managed but prioritized. Too often, the belief is that time can be managed like people. However, that isn't the case—I can prioritize what I do with my time, but I cannot slow time down or speed time up. Consider this, when you are late for a meeting and sit at a stop light for a few minutes, those minutes seem like twenty or thirty. However, when spending time doing things you love, those few minutes go by quick. If I could manage time, I would speed up or slow down time like I can do when listening to an audiobook on my mobile device. However, when I adjust the playback speed of audio, the sound is distorted compared to the original. That is the same thing that happens when people attempt to manage time. Time becomes distorted. Just like the driver that believed they could do two things at once, they distorted the time it took to do each activity. Which ultimately caused my death and a new life."

"Wow! I, I, never thought of time in this manner. Um, I never asked, do you have children? Are those kids you were playing with your children?" Michael asked.

"No, unfortunately, I didn't always think this way, and early in my marriage, we were both consumed with our careers. Living life together but apart. I worked for a large company and spent too much time doing things that—um, were not the best activities for raising a family or being married. Betty Sue isn't my first wife, but she is my best wife. My first wife and I split after—well some of the stuff I did surfaced. It wasn't long after we separated that I was in the accident I mentioned and it wasn't far from the main intersection, minutes off the interstate, not far from Nana's diner. I was on my way home from a business meeting and growing tired and pulled off the interstate to find a place to get some food and coffee. Well, you know some of the rest of the story.

"While in the hospital, John, Nana's husband, came to visit me. Obviously, this was before he passed. I couldn't understand why someone that I didn't know would visit me in what I thought was a forsaken little town. At first, I thought he wanted something. Maybe a job or money, but then I got to know him. Not real talkative, I think Nana did most of the talking for both of them. He would sit with me saying little, but just wanted to be there in the event I needed help. Then one day—it seemed like out of nowhere, he asked, 'Are you living a life worth remembering? You are in the hospital bed feeling sorry for yourself, but miss that you were given a second chance at this thing called life.'

"I looked at him and almost told him to get out. I was offended. Here I was in a hospital bed recovering from 'dying,' and he asked this question. I am sure my blood pressure caused the machine to spike. Yes, I was angry and feeling sorry for myself. I was in a horrible car accident, died, and looked like I was in a fight with a she-bear and lost. But, I waited, and he continued. 'If you remained dead at the scene, would anyone remember that you lived? Are you living a life that impacts others for the better? Are you using the time wisely given to you by our creator? Are you going to do something with the second chance you were given?.'

> "Are you living a life that impacts others for the better?"

"His words stopped my tongue from moving. I remember thinking, my parents are passed, and my ex would cry for a few minutes, but then rejoice when she received the insurance check. My work 'family' would forget me the minute they hired a replacement and tossed my 'stuff' in the trash. I responded 'NO' so loud to his questions that one of the nurses ran into the room. John had to convince them I was okay. After they checked my vitals and scolded both of us, the nurse left the room but did come back to check on me every ten or fifteen minutes for the next hour. I always laugh when I think back how they would poke their head in the room to check on us. John was sitting calmly on the chair, and I was sitting there with a massive grin on my face. What a sight.

"John showed me that not only was I given a second chance at life, but my duty and obligation was to do something with it. He stated that he heard a statement once but didn't know where it originated. 'It isn't the years you live but the life you live in those years.' Many people die young but live a much fuller life than those who live eighty plus years but do nothing outside their four walls. He kept stating, 'don't quit on life or people, it is easy to quit and lay in that bed feeling sorry for yourself, but there is someone out there that must hear your story.'"

"After getting over feeling sorry for myself and realizing the truth in John's statements, I changed my habits, what I did daily, and ultimately, my life. I received a settlement from the accident, left my day gig, and fortunately met Betty Sue.

"Back to your question. The kids are nieces and nephews, plus a few children from the neighborhood. Betty Sue and I can't have kids, and we talked about adopting, but never did and enjoy spending time with other folks' kids. I love kids, but also love giving them back, which is why we don't have pets either. We both enjoy travel, and often she will attend conferences around the world where I do talks. She is the numbers person and keeps our business in the black. I would give everything away, but we are a great balance since she isn't as outgoing as me. I keep her in the social world, and she keeps me from living in my truck."

"On a serious note, did you know there are 1440 minutes in a day? How are you using them in pursuit of your life goals?" Robbie asked.

Michael almost missed the question, he was so engrossed in Robbie's conversation. "Huh?"

"There are 1440 minutes per day with no chance to borrow from yesterday. If you fail to use them wisely, you can't pull minutes from your tomorrow. The closing statement from most of my talks is the same. How are you using your 1440?"

"Wow! I never thought of a day in that manner . . ." As Michael was talking, Abby joined them, and Michael continued. "This is my wife, Abby. Abby, this is Robbie. Betty Sue's husband. The comptroller Nana mentioned."

"Nice to meet you," Abby said.

"Nice to meet you too. Here is my information and something to consider," Robbie said as he handed a note card to Michael.

"I need to finish a football game with some kids. It was great chatting with you, Michael. If you ever want to talk more, send me a note or find me on social media," Robbie said as he ran toward the others playing in the field.

Michael looked at the card and read:

'Your1440Today.com How are you using your 1440 minutes today?'

You cannot purchase time - time has a value far more significant than money.

What is it that you want out of life?

If you knew you couldn't fail, would you do more?

If you knew you couldn't fail, would you put off doing what you should do today?

If you believed in yourself, would you dream bigger?

"You have 1440 minutes per day, please use it wisely."

Michael took Abby's hand in his, and they walked toward the lake and setting sun.

CHAPTER NINETEEN

Finding a bench near the lake, Abby and Michael sat on it facing the setting sun. Abby put her head on Michael's shoulder and whispered, "What a day!"

Michael said, "What a weekend!"

They both laughed.

"What are we going to do with what we learned?" Michael asked. "How do we ensure that we don't forget what we learned and what are we going to do with us? Our family? Our lives? I know I don't need to ask, but have you checked on the kids lately?"

With a gentle push, Abby said, "Yes, my aunt put them in a closet, and they are playing video games."

"Yea, right!"

"I checked with her not long ago, and they were getting cleaned up and ready for bed. They have a busy day planned for tomorrow, and with the holiday, she said they were going to a parade in the city."

"Good, maybe we can go for a walk in the morning," Michael suggested. "I would like to thank Officer Dan, Ginnie, and all of the others for their hospitality. They might be busy, though, since their son came home. What do you make of that?"

"That sounds like a plan," Abby said. "I don't know. I didn't want to pry, but I couldn't stop watching them. I wonder what happened to him and where had he been that he arrived looking like a—homeless person?"

"Yea, earlier in the weekend, I thought Officer Dan, Nana, and their families were 'perfect', but Nana said they had a child that had issues and it appears Dan and Ginnie has one too," Michael said. "It makes me feel better, sorta. I mean, if everything were perfect in their lives, then I would wonder if what they said was possible for us. Something keeps coming to my mind that no one here said, but I remember it from a book I read, I think it is an African Proverb. 'It takes a village to raise a child.' But what I learned is it takes a village to grow as a person, and we cannot live in hibernation. We need to find some new friends."

Abby responded without hesitation. "We need more than new friends. We need friends that lift us up rather than tear us down. Grandma always said, 'hang out with good kids because you become whom you play with.' I am sorry that I listened to Stella. Deep down, I knew you were not having an affair, but what she said and the way she said it made it possible in my mind."

Michael squeezed Abby tight to him. They sat in silence, watching the ducks swim off into the sunset, creating a beautiful ending to the night.

A few minutes later, they heard someone approach from behind and turning they saw Zoe standing with a big smile on her face and camera in hand.

"You two love birds enjoying the sunset too? I love coming here and watching the sky turn all colors, and it reminds me that the day is ending here, but somewhere else in the world, it is just starting new. My favorite activity is to rise early, and venture out toward the waterfall and watch the sun rise over it. The peaceful sounds of the water combined with the glow of the sun glistening is memorizing, creating a trance-like effect.

"My parents wanted me to ask you to join them and a few others at the main house mid-morning if possible," Zoe continued. "They--we were not sure when you planned to go home and want to say goodbye. They are having a small brunch in celebration of my brother coming home and—I'm

CHAPTER NINETEEN

sorry," Zoe wiped tears from her cheeks. "It isn't going to be anything big, not like tonight, just a few friends and family. I mean, if it's okay with you. What I mean, if you feel like spending some more time with us." She rushed over to them, gave them a big hug, then ran off toward the cart path.

Abby and Michael stood as Zoe ran off, then looked to each other, wiping the tears from the other's cheeks.

CHAPTER TWENTY

Abby woke to the songs of birds and light streaming in through the window in the bedroom.

I love how she touches me and rubs my back. Her warmth and the sweet smell of her perfume are pleasant to wake to each morning. Why do I spend so much time away when she brings so much joy to me?

Leaning over to kiss Michael while massaging his back, she said, "Rise and shine—I Went To Sleep Last Night With A Smile Because I Knew I'd Be Dreaming Of You—And I Woke Up This Morning With A Smile Because You Weren't A Dream."

"Where did you read that?" Michael asked.

"I just made it up!" Abby said. She was laughing as she attempted to tickle Michael.

"Yea, right! But I like it even though I know you read it somewhere." He pulled her to him and nearly fell off the twin bed as they continued to laugh and kiss.

They laid in each other's arms for a few more minutes resting in the comfort and security of their time together.

"I read in a magazine that if you kiss me every morning, you will live longer," Abby said.

"Really?" Michael asked.

"No, but it sure beats the alternative of not kissing me, and let's try it daily to see if it works."

"Let's go for a hike. Show me where you met Sensei," Abby suggested.

"Okay, it looks like a nice morning," Michael said as he looked through the curtains in the bedroom.

CHAPTER TWENTY

Grabbing the go bag from the closet, packing some fruit, water and a small inflatable life preserver from a shelf, Michael and Abby headed toward the rising sun and waterfall. Knowing his way, Michael navigated the two of them through the trees and underbrush with ease.

Michael thought, *I like this, getting out with Abby. How did I forget how wonderful it felt to be with her walking in the sunlight and enjoying God's creation?*

Nearing the embankment leading to the waterfall, Michael reached out his hand to take Abby's and helped her down the embankment.

"Wow! This is more amazing than I imagined. I wish we could visit here every morning to see the sun paint beautiful colors in the sky and it glisten off the spraying water. I love the sunrise more than a sunset as the birds sing, the morning air warms after a cool evening, and it reminds us that The Lord provides us with a new day to do something to help others." Abby said.

"Who are you? Where did you come up with all of this stuff?" Michael asked.

"Actually, this weekend brought out things that were suppressed by our crazy life. When I was little, and before we moved away from Grandma, I would stand at the street corner waiting for the bus and see her working in her yard, trimming grass with a pair of scissors around immaculate flower beds and small statues of cartoon characters. I always thought it was crazy how early she got up to work in the yard, kneeling in the dew covered grass, and singing songs in a high off-pitched voice. She would sing so loud and off-pitch that I think the psalmist was thinking of her when he wrote, 'make a joyful noise unto the LORD'. She would see me, stand up, wave, and say something about the sunrise telling me that the good Lord provided me with a new day, and it was my duty to do something with it," Abby said.

"I never understood her love for mornings until now. I've been too busy with life to enjoy each morning. I, I mean, we need to teach our kids to enjoy each morning as a gift from God. She used to say that the previous generations thought nothing of rising early in the morning to do the things that needed to be done. Then she would laugh and say, 'when I think of it, this generation thinks nothing of it either'. I tried to understand what she meant, but now I appreciate what she said. We don't get up and enjoy the morning, we might 'get up,' but we don't enjoy the sunrise and be still while we listen to the birds sing, the wind rustles through the trees, and all of the beautiful sounds provided to us in nature.

"Another favorite saying she said to me on the weekends, 'Some folks don't realize that the sun gradually appears in the sky. They think it just shows up.' I yearn for the days when life was simpler. Michael, we need to make a change. I know that you love what you do and you make excellent money, but we need to get to know each other again. We must be friends again. I am not the enemy when I tell you that I miss you or that you need to spend more time at home. Too bad you can't work from home." Abby sighed as she leaned over and kissed Michael on his lips, noticing a small tear on his cheek. Wiping it away, she kissed him several more times.

Abby reached for the bag to get some water, but instead of grabbing the bag's strap, she grabbed the cord for the life preserver causing it to begin inflating within the bag then popping out hitting them both on the head, knocking them back, causing them to laugh. They rolled around, laughing and giggling like two teenagers in love.

Her touch. Her softness. Her trust.

"Abby, I am so sorry! I don't know what happened, but something caused me to lose focus on the real me. I am good at what I do and actually enjoy it, but I don't love it, nor do

CHAPTER TWENTY

I believe that I am impacting people the way I should. The work that I do takes me away from the people I love the most on earth, and I don't find fulfillment and I, I, I take out my frustration on you and the kids—"

Interrupting, Abby said, "I forgive you."

"Yes, but I need to forgive me and just as important, I need to make a change and do something different, but I don't know what to do. We have lots of debt and payments. The only way we can pay for what we have is for me to stay in my current job—"

Michael's mind recalled the day he walked around Lamar's garage and then drifted to the many nights he worked with his dad building, rebuilding, and dreaming. *What caused me to get off the correct path? Was I ever on it?* Staring off into space, Michael thought. *How do I fix this mess?*

"Michael, Michael, hello earth to Michael," Abby said.

Abby was looking directly into Michael's eyes. "Show me the cave where Gabriel came out of nowhere, and you hit your head."

"You want to see where I hit my head?" Michael said.

"No, I said that to make sure you were listening," Abby teased.

Taking Abby by the hand, Michael guided Abby to the cave. They sat with their legs dangling over the edge. Putting her head on Michael's, Abby said, "This is beautiful. You know we can sell everything and start life fresh. We can buy something smaller. The kids will adapt, we can—We will adapt."

"Yes, and we must. Thank you for walking by my side on this journey called life. When I was in college, I had a professor that always said, 'When the student is ready, the teacher will appear.' He didn't know where the saying originated, but it stuck in my mind. This weekend proved the saying. I, I mean, we were ready and wow did the teachers appear. I am sure it wasn't by 'chance' that I fell asleep in an area that would call Officer Dan to wake me up and investigate me. He could have been a jerk, but after verifying that I was 'harmless', he showed kindness and mercy. Nor do I think it was chance that Lamar came to this area years ago, that Officer Dan took me to see him, and I saw a replica of the Z28 like the one my dad and I rebuilt. I don't think it was chance that caused you to visit Grandma and for Zoe to help Officer Dan and Ginnie bring you to me. We were both ready as students, and the teachers appeared. As if out of nowhere but they were here all the time. But we were not ready for it. I wasn't prepared for Gabriel to appear in this opening and the lump on my head proves that . . ."

"Poor baby!" Abby said as she rubbed Michael's head. "Do you want me to kiss it and make it feel better?"

"Yes!" Michael said.

"I'll kiss your lips instead," Abby said.

"Now, where was I?" Michael asked.

"You were sitting next to me telling me how beautiful I look and how wonderful I am to come here with you," Abby joked.

Rolling his eyes, Michael said, "You are more beautiful to me today than the first day I laid eyes on you for more reasons than physical beauty. Maybe we can bring the kids here soon and . . . "

Glancing at his watch, Michael said, "Wow! Look at the time. We need to get to brunch. I don't want them to think we stood them up and left or something."

"Yes, we need to bring the kids here and show them that we can be fun and enjoy life. They wouldn't think we left. Your vehicle is at the cabin," Abby said.

Standing, they looked at the falls marveling in its majestic power and sounds.

CHAPTER TWENTY

Michael said, "Be careful. The wind is spraying water from the falls on the stones . . ." As Michael put his left foot on a stone, he realized it was a mistake, and he fell back and started a fast descent down the more than one hundred foot grade toward the base of the falls.

I need to stop! I am heading dead on to a tree.

Attempting to stop his fall, he reached out and grabbed a sapling, but it did nothing to slow his fall and caused him to hit the side of a small tree which propelled him toward the deeper side of the creek. When he hit the tree with his side, he felt the air get knocked out of him. As he continued the slide, he grabbed for anything and tried to dig his heels into the mud, but to no avail.

"Ugh! My arm, my ribs!"

When Michael slipped, at first Abby thought he was playing and said, "Stop playing around! You are going to get hurt!" Then when she realized he was plunging into the raging waters near the base of the falls, she started screaming, "Help! Someone help!"

"Michael! Michael!" she screamed.

As Michael reached the base of the hill, his left foot caught on a stump causing his body to twist, and he heard his ankle pop as the intense pain ran up his entire leg. When he hit the frigid water, he gasped from the cold and cried out: "Oh, God, help me! Abby, please protect Abby!"

Still gasping for air after his collision with the tree, combined with the shock of the cold water, he took in a mouth full of muddy water. He was then drug under from the speed of his fall and the undercurrent from the waterfall. Thrashing his arms to stay above the water, he could hear Abby screaming for help when he was pulled under again. His head hit the base of a tree, and the world went black.

"Help! Help! Someone help!" Abby screamed as she stood watching Michael slide down the hill then go under water. She began to cry, frantically calling for help. Then out of the woods to her left, she saw a man in army khakis and sleeveless shirt come out of the woods racing toward the spot where she last saw Michael before he went under water. In a controlled manner, the man slid down the hill toward the water, then when the man reached the spot Michael went into the water, he slid in and was gone for seconds, but to Abby, it seemed like an eternity.

Seconds later, the man emerged covered with mud all through his hair and beard and Michael in his arms. Placing him gently on the ground, he began performing CPR alternating between rescue breaths and chest compressions. The man yelled to Abby. "Call my mom!"

"Your mom? Who's your mom?"

Between rescue breaths, he responded.

"Ginnie, call Ginnie and tell her to get a four by four to the falls fast, then call Dr. Luke!"

Abby grabbed the go bag and dug through it, finding her phone, and as she pulled it out, she dropped it as her hands shook in fear.

"What's her number?"

The man yelled the number and continued performing CPR—"Stay with me, man! Stay with me!"

Abby's hands continued to shake as she attempted to dial the number.

I can't see!

Wiping her eyes with her hands to see the screen through her tears, she tapped in the number.

"Oh God, help. Ginnie, please answer the phone."

After the third ring, Ginnie answered.

"Ginnie! Ginnie!" Abby shouted between sobs.

"Michael—Michael. He fell, he's hurt, he went under water! I think he drowned! A man told me to call you. . . Help me! Help us!" As Abby backed into the cave, she nearly collapsed from the strain.

CHAPTER TWENTY

Ginnie attempted to console Abby telling her to slow down and tell her their location.

"A man—he is helping Michael. I think he is dead! No, not the man. Michael. I think he . . ."

She continued frantically. "He, the man, your son, said to tell you to meet us at the falls with a four by four and call Dr. Luke."

Just then, Abby heard the man shout. "That's it, cough out the mud and water. Abby, do you have a bottle of water? If so, toss it to me carefully! Michael is breathing, but he is hurt and needs help! Are my mom and dad on their way?"

The rescuer noticed the go bag and recognized it from the cabin where he stayed many nights. Hoping it had a small IFAK (individual first aid kit), he said, "Throw me the go bag. I will use the stuff in it and the bag to prop his head."

"Ginnie, please hurry!" Abby screamed into the phone.

"Okay, okay. Thank you!" Abby said into the phone, then hit the end call button, and she called out to the rescuer.

"She said they would be here soon!" She continued to sob uncontrollably.

"God, we need your help!"

Ten minutes later, three four-wheel drive vehicles with multiple men Abby didn't know, plus Ginnie, Zoe, and Officer Dan arrived and navigated their way toward Michael carrying a stretcher and other medical aid. Ginnie and Zoe went to Abby, wrapped a blanket around her while they attempted to calm and reassure her that everything would be okay.

The men placed Michael on the stretcher, strapped him onto it then carried him toward the vehicles. After carefully securing him in the back of Officer Dan's truck, Officer Dan, Ginnie, and one of the men sped off with a magnetically mounted police flasher on Officer Dan's truck.

CHAPTER TWENTY-ONE

Zoe and Abby climbed into a jeep with two of the men and Christopher, the man who rescued Michael, scrambled into the back, barely fitting into the tight space behind the back seat. As they raced off behind Officer Dan and Ginnie, Abby looked back to the man covered with mud and said, "Thank you! I don't know your name, nor have we been formally introduced."

Reaching out his hand toward Abby to shake her hand, he said, "Ma'am, my name is Christopher. I am Ginnie and Dan's son. It is my pleasure to meet you, but I wish—I wish our meeting were under different circumstances. From what I can tell, your husband will be okay. He is hurt, but he will be okay."

Abby noticed the tattoos on his muscular right arm, covering it from the wrist to his shoulder with what appeared to be images of people with names and dates under them. Then she noticed his other arm was the same and there was a notable scar on the left side of his face that started under his ear and toward the front of his throat. It stopped under his jawline, and it stood out since his beard didn't grow over the scar. She studied his face, which wasn't intimidating, and his eyes were filled with compassion. His mud covered hair was long and pulled back behind his head which was wrapped in a bandana with an emblem she didn't recognize, and his arms, shirt, and pants were covered with mud.

"How did you know what to do back there, where did you come from? How did you find us, are you the same man

CHAPTER TWENTY-ONE

that was at the picnic last night?" Abby rambled without taking a breath.

Smiling, the man said in a calm voice. "Ma'am, I did a few tours in the sandbox and had to rescue—tried to rescue. I served in the military, Special Forces, and unfortunately, I've seen worse conditions. Things that no one should see ever." He paused for a few minutes, and Abby could tell it was causing him pain to think about it. He turned from Abby and gazed out the back window of the Jeep.

Zoe interjected to help her brother. "My brother is a war hero, and at times struggles with what he saw during his time in the war." Zoe started to cry, and Christopher came to his sister's aid.

"Yep, since I came home, life's tossed me a few challenges. The memories haunt me. The men and woman that—didn't make it. Why did I make it, but they didn't? Why me?"

Abby pointed to some of the tattoos on his arms and asked, "Are those some of your friends?"

Christopher pointed with his mud covered left hand to his large upper right arm where it read, 'Never Forget'.

"The tats on my arms are some of the comrades I fought with but didn't come back. Others I have on my bike. It is a small memorial, a reminder for me to go on. It isn't always easy. When I am clean, I ride it. The last few months have been tough, and I fell off the wagon, but my family and friends are always there to pick me up and help me through the nightmares. I am glad I was able to put to use some of my training to help you and your husband. To answer your other questions. Actually, you speak faster and louder than some of my drill sergeants."

This statement caused Abby to smile as she wiped tears from her eyes. "I get that way when I am scared and nervous."

"Ma'am, no need to apologize."

"Please, you don't need to call me ma'am. We are nearly the same age."

"Yes, ma'am," Christopher said, which caused them all to laugh.

"My mom sent me to find the two of you since we were getting ready to have brunch," Zoe said.

"Brunch! Oh no! We ruined your brunch! I am so sorry," Abby said as she put her head in her hands.

Christopher looked to his sister and mouthed, "I think she needs a big hug from you."

Zoe put her arms around Abby and said, "It's okay, all that matters is Michael, and you are fine."

Minutes later, they pulled into a parking lot behind a row of offices.

The driver, an older man, turned to Zoe and said, "Your dad said to drop you all here and call your mom when you arrive. The office is closed today, but Doc came in to help the young man. If you need anything else, please have your mom or dad call me. I am going to go to the diner and get a few things from Nana; she went there when we got the call, but wants to come here now."

Zoe, Abby, and Christopher exited the Jeep, and they thanked the man multiple times for the ride.

Ginnie was waiting at the front door and barely able to contain herself, Abby ran toward it, "How is Michael?"

"He will be fine! Doc ran preliminary tests on him, and all indications are he will suffer no more than bruised ribs and will need crutches for his ankle. We are running a few more tests, and Doc is attending to him now. The three of you stay in the waiting room, and I will get you when you can visit with him."

The entire trip to the doctor's office, Michael kept asking about Abby. Ginnie did her best to calm him down.

CHAPTER TWENTY-ONE

When they arrived, Ginnie said, "Doc, thank you for coming in. We were not sure of his condition, and it is nearly 40 minutes more to the hospital."

Dr. Luke looked at Officer Dan and the other man who looked as if he could carry Michael on his own. "Bring him in. Ginnie and I will get started with the needed tests after she cleans up."

CHAPTER TWENTY-TWO

Thirty minutes later, the doctor walked into Michael's room.

"Michael, you are one blessed man," Doc said. "Your ribs are bruised, and your ankle is sprained, but neither the ribs nor ankle are broken. The scans I did on your head don't show anything wrong."

"Yep, that would be about right. Abby always says I am hard headed and often wonders if there is anything between my ears. Saying things go in one ear and out the other." Michael said.

"What I mean is, you don't show signs of a concussion," the doctor continued, ignoring Michael's attempt at humor. "You took on some dirty water, I gave you some antibiotics and did tests, but I think you should get a few tests completed at the hospital for your head. All indications show you don't have a concussion, but I would rather be safe than sorry. My office is small, and I am not equipped for more extensive testing. I will write you a prescription for some more medicine and order the tests. Nana called and asked about you. Your wife, Zoe, and Christopher are waiting to see you. Before I let them in, I wanted to talk to you man to man. Not doctor to patient."

"Um, Okay, sure. Go ahead." Michael was unsure what to expect.

"Nana asked if I could talk to you about how I ended up in this town."

"Wow! Everyone I meet here seems to have a story."

"Yes, you would be correct in that observation," Doc said. "Have you ever heard of the golden handcuffs?"

CHAPTER TWENTY-TWO

"Golden handcuffs? No? What does it mean?" Michael asked.

"The term, 'golden handcuffs' is often used to describe when a person has a great job or gig going, but it isn't exactly what they want, but to leave is foolish because of either pay, working conditions, benefits, and or a combination of all three and more. I didn't start my medical practice in this town but was a high-priced doctor in New York City with a clientele of pro athletes, actors, and actresses, singers, and an income and side benefits that would stagger your mind and would seem unbelievable. My wife and I were living in luxury, and we loved the life New York City provided.

"The stress was getting to me, but we were so accustomed to living 'high on the hog' that neither of us considered anything different for years. Then one day, out of nowhere, my wife said that she was tired of the fast pace, insane expectations, and non-stop pace of a big city doctor's wife. I told her that we couldn't give up our life. I didn't want to give up our lifestyle. We had multiple six-figure luxury cars, a penthouse, a summer house, and enough antiques and collectibles to open a gallery. Unfortunately, we argued about it every few weeks. Then it was weekly, and finally, it turned into a daily battle. She couldn't take it and told me I needed to decide if I wanted the 'stuff' or her. I argued that we both had an intense dream to live this lifestyle since my days in medical school, and she agreed. I dedicated myself to my profession, and the devotion provided me skills that many didn't possess.

"But she said she was growing tired and didn't want it any longer. I kept telling her she needed a vacation and to spend some time away while I made a few decisions. When she came back from her vacation, she said she didn't feel any better. This information concerned me, I had been too busy to notice her symptoms and contacted a colleague to run tests on her for me. I didn't want to run them so

TWO ARE BETTER THAN ONE

I wasn't distracted or tainted in my professional opinion. Unfortunately, she was ill. Very ill. I won't go into the details, but I missed the signs because I was chained to a world that I created with golden handcuffs. What we had wasn't wrong, but I missed the signs that my wife was ill because I let the world I created, flaw my vision. I was sick over it for many reasons. All of my skill and money couldn't save her. All of my contacts and friends couldn't stop the inevitable—her death. She lived a few more months.

"I was crushed and fell into a deep depression and didn't know what to do. We never had children. Ginnie and I are second cousins, and after my wife died, Ginnie suggested I sell everything and move to this town to relax and start fresh. At first, I refused, but then Nana called, and she is one persistent woman! She kept calling until I agreed on spending a few weeks here. I stayed at the cottage on Ginnie and Dan's property. The few weeks turned into me returning every other weekend for a few months. I decided that I needed to start fresh, sold my practice, the two places we owned, and all of the antiques. I did keep the one Benz, it was my wife's, and well, I couldn't sell it. I bought the property this building is on and rented the other four offices in the complex to other professionals. Ginnie, a trained and experienced nurse, worked with me when I started my practice here and every so often, she will help me when one of my staff needs time off. As I started to say, I rented the other offices to professionals, and one of them is a lawyer. She and I started dating and the wildest thing—her story is similar to mine, and we are getting married next year.

"Michael, you were given a second chance at life. I don't know what you do nor the life you live. But Nana felt it important that I tell you the story about the golden handcuffs. We all have choices to make in life, and my gut is telling me you need to make a choice about certain things in life..."

CHAPTER TWENTY-TWO

A knock on the door interrupted them. Ginnie poked her head in the room. "Doc, I am sorry, but I will need to give Abby a sedative soon if she doesn't at least see Michael."

"Let her in. We can give them some time, and the others can visit too. He is fine, a little bruised and battered, but he is young," He slapped Michael on the shoulder as he smiled. "Christopher did a great job in his rescue. Be sure to tell your son he did a good job!"

"I will," Ginnie said as she closed the door.

CHAPTER TWENTY-THREE

Abby raced into the room and nearly knocked Michael off the small bed where he was sitting.

"I thought I lost you!" She kissed him all over his face and gave him a long hug.

Wincing from the pain in his ribs from the bear-like hug, Michael pulled back.

"Oh, I hurt you," Abby said.

"No, I am fine. We are fine!" Michael reassured her.

Sitting on the chair next to him, Abby told him about Christopher, how he came out of nowhere, and what she learned during their trip to the doctor's office, and on and on she went. Michael put up his right hand and placed his hand gently on her lips and said.

"I am good. Do I need to have Doc give you something to calm you down?"

"Noooo! You scared me! I thought I lost you!" she said.

Michael took Abby's closest hand in his and lifted them and kissed her hand. "Can you introduce me to Christopher?"

"Oh, how thoughtless of me. I will get him and Zoe. No doubt, they are very anxious to see you. I will go get them."

"I will wait here."

Not acknowledging his sarcasm, Abby left the room then came back in and blew him a kiss.

A few minutes later, the room was filled with Zoe, Nana, and Abby. Officer Dan and Ginnie waited in the receiving area of the doctor's office.

CHAPTER TWENTY-THREE

When Nana entered, she was followed by Christopher, who carried a crock-pot filled with food, and its aroma filled the room with smells of bacon, sausage, and eggs.

"Don't tell Doc that we have this food, but I am sure you are hungry!" Nana said.

She told Christopher to place the crock-pot on a table near the window and opened the crockpot, revealing biscuit sandwiches, bacon, and enough sausage to feed a small army.

"Michael, Michael, Michael!" Nana exclaimed. "What are we going to do with you? What are you going to do with you? When are we going to meet your children? Will you come to visit us after you heal?"

"Our children!" Abby cried out. "I need to call my aunt and tell her we will be late tonight!" Abby said as she ran out of the room.

"That poor woman, we need to have doc giver her one of those 'relaxatives' and keep her away from that iced coffee," Nana said as she shook her head and laughed. "Well? Will we get to meet your children? What are you going to do with you?" Nana asked with her hands on her hips.

"I think I need an attorney to intercede for me during this interrogation. Where are Doc and his fiancé?" Michael said as he started laughing.

Nana began serving sandwiches on paper plates with plastic ware that she had in a bag. Out of a small cooler, Christopher handed out bottles of iced coffee. Officer Dan and Ginnie joined them and brought a few chairs from a neighboring room.

"Yes, we will bring our children to visit. As for what I intend to do, I know I need to make many changes. When I was sliding down the hill and went underwater, I was afraid. Not for me, but Abby and our children. I was not afraid to die but . . ." Wiping tears from his eyes, Michael continued.

"Abby is a good woman. She has stood by me in good and bad times. I need help in making a change. Maybe a counselor or—what are some of them called? Zoe, what did you call your friend?—A life coach?" Said Michael.

"Yes, Ebony is a life coach," Zoe affirmed.

"Yes, I need to find someone in my area that I can meet with to help me through this process of change. I heard a few folks tell me that two are better than one, and I need a coach to guide me and hold me accountable for my actions and decisions. Someone said that not making a decision is actually making a decision not to change, and I need help changing," Michael said.

As Michael was talking, Abby walked into the room and stuffed her phone in her pocket. As she did so, she felt something else in her pocket. She pulled out a piece of paper and realized it was the paper she read the day before at the cabin.

Attempting to straighten it, she said, "I found this in the cabin. Do any of you know this 'Dr. Frank'? This paper looks like it is from a book or seminar."

Zoe said, "Yes, he is good friends with Ebony. He is a speaker and author, plus a great photographer. They met at a conference where he was speaking. He used to hold photo walks regularly. I attended one not far from here and had a great time, learning more than photography. He has a story for everything. I mean, here we are taking pictures of butterflies and the next thing he had a bunch of us in a circle talking about the butterfly effect and how every one of us will impact others. Some in a positive manner and others in a negative manner. Then he ended with one of his corny dad like jokes. 'Everyone makes a positive impact on others. Some when they enter the room and others when they leave.' I can get you his information from Ebony; I think he has a website too."

Abby said, "That would be great!"

"Oh, . . . If that's okay with you, Michael."

CHAPTER TWENTY-THREE

Laughing and pulling his wife close to him, Michael agreed. "It would be great. Great for both of us to do together. As a team."

Everyone in the room laughed, and they talked for another hour while they finished eating the food.

Michael said. "I—we want to thank you for all of your hospitality, love, and support. Officer Dan, thank you for showing me mercy the first day we met. Nana, thank you for your food and directness. I mean, you are direct and to the point. Thank you! I can go on and on, but we will be back with our children and take you up on your offers."

Abby gave him a tight squeeze then stopped when she realized Michael winced with pain from his bruised ribs.

Officer Dan said, "Yep, my mom, Nana, is direct and to the point, and we love her because of it."

Nana laughed and while looking to Office Dan said, "My directness kept you in line, and I think you came out okay."

Giving his mom a side to side hug, Officer Dan said. "Yep, we need to get going. Michael, Doc said you are good to go. Ginnie brought you a pair of khakis and a pull-over shirt. They are in the paper bag on the window sill. We will give you a few minutes to change and will be outside to take you back to the cabin."

As everyone was leaving, Christopher said, "I will be out in a few minutes. Give me a few minutes with Michael and Abby.—I just—I would like to talk to them."

CHAPTER TWENTY-FOUR

After the others left the room, Christopher said, "I am not good at telling. I mean, I don't do good with…"

Wiping tears from his cheek, Christopher said, "It's sorta ironic. I have jumped out of planes, ran into burning buildings to rescue fellow soldiers, but talking about this life lesson stuff is tough for me. I am like my dad. We like to do rather than tell."

Abby and Michael waited as Christopher composed himself, then started again. "I don't have a lot of stuff. Actually, I don't have any stuff except a duffle bag of clothes, my bike, a small bag of tools, and a few other things. However, I am blessed with an amazing circle of friends and family. This makes me rich beyond anything money can buy. I don't know much about the two of you other than what I heard today. I am not passing judgment."

Christopher paused and looked out the window for a few seconds.

"I have seen things that—things that caused the wires in my head to detach and I do—did things that brought pain to my life and my family. I don't like to talk about it, but the pain in my head caused me to drink too much, and I got addicted to prescription drugs. I am blessed because I have friends and family that always welcome me home with open arms and to me, that's priceless."

Christopher paused, composing his thoughts. "My perspective on life changed when I went to war and came home. Not all of us did—I mean, come home. I used to take life for granted. I always worked out, strength and

CHAPTER TWENTY-FOUR

size came naturally for me. I ate, lifted weights, and grew big. Thinking I was invincible, almost able to stop bullets, knives, and bombs with my hands." As Christopher said these last words, his fingers on his left hand kept running up and down the scar on the side of his face that ran under the jawline. "Before I went to fight for our country, I gave mom and dad a tough time. Being the biggest, I thought I needed to be the toughest too. I caused my parents many sleepless nights."

Christopher took a drink of water from a water bottle, then continued. "I no longer take life for granted and do my best to make every minute count. I messed up a few times. Like recently. There are times when the nightmares are not nightmares but occur in the day. And—life is made up of many chapters. My parents are nothing short of amazing. The stuff I put them through. Let's say they have a special dose of grace and mercy. It has been said that a soldier sacrifices his life for his country for freedom's sake and while my family and friends keep me going, there is One Greater—I am forever reminded of a greater Man that made the ultimate sacrifice – for my soul and life."

Taking another drink from the water bottle and wiping his mouth with the back of his hand, Christopher continued. "I don't want to sound preachy or anything. But there were times I wanted to quit. I could have quit many times, and I don't think too many would fault me. My faith in God kept me going. We had a great chaplain in the service. He kept at us, pointing us in the right direction when—when things were bad. I mean real bad. My family and friends stood by me. When I fell, they picked me up. Life hit me hard, but no harder than life hit you today. I mean, if I hadn't gone through stuff—if I didn't understand the value of life—maybe I wouldn't have been as inclined to help you, but I know the value of each breath. What I mean is my folks didn't quit on me, and I think you will value life more now than you did last week. I ain't judging you or anything, but don't quit. I am not saying that you would. You have a good thing going. From what I see, the two of you love each other. You have kids, a family, stuff folks want. I never married, but maybe one day I will. I pray that I find a lady that loves me like Abby loves you, and my mom loves my dad.

"I ah, I hope you come back to visit with us. Maybe you can meet some of the others that helped me in my life—there are some of us—we get together and one of the guys—he leads a Bible study. We study God's word—Scriptures—I mean—it helps more than I can explain. You need to experience it."

Abby got up and walked over to Christopher, hugging him, and said, "Thank you for everything you did. Not only today but in your life. How you served our great nation and put your skills and heart into saving Michael. We would be honored to come back and meet the others."

Michael reached out his hand, giving Christopher a handshake and tried pulling him in for a hug, but Christopher's size caused Michael to stop, then Christopher pulled Michael to him in a firm, but gentle embrace.

"Thank you!" Michael said. "Thank you for risking your life for your country yesterday and today for me. I owe you my life and will be back to meet your friends. It is the least that I could do. I can never fully repay you for what you did, but I want to know more about what you said."

Clearing his throat and pointing over his right shoulder with his right thumb, Christopher said, "Um, I gotta go—there are a few guys I need to meet up with and—sir, ma'am, it has been an honor. When you come back, we can do some guy stuff, things where I am more comfortable, and we can chat more. Maybe we can build something. I am really good at that stuff. My mom's dad was a carpenter. When he was alive, he taught me how to use my hands and mind to build

CHAPTER TWENTY-FOUR

and fix things. Maybe I can show you the stone and cedar cabin we built the year before he passed."

Christopher stood and started to leave the room then turned to Michael and Abby.

"Abby, if it is okay with you. Will you give Michael and me a few minutes alone? I would like to talk to him—guy to guy. If it's okay with you ma'am."

"Yea, sure. I will wait outside with your mom."

After Abby left the room, Christopher pulled a chair up next to the bed turning the back of the chair toward Michael and sitting facing him with his arms leaning on the top of the chair.

"Michael, I couldn't leave without talking to you and asking you a few critical questions. You almost died earlier today. From the little I can see, you have a good life, and you almost lost it. Life could end fast. A few weeks ago—a few weeks ago, I lost a good buddy of mine. There were a bunch of us guys riding our Harleys, and we were riding on the main road outside town to get some ice cream. Out of nowhere, a little kid on one of those battery-powered plastic toys that look like a truck came out of a driveway onto the main road in front of Larry. I was a few bikes back from Larry and saw the scene unfolding in front of my eyes and started yelling for the kid to stop. Larry must have seen the kid and swerved left and hit some gravel on the road, causing him to slide, then his front tire hit a pothole." Christopher paused as he looked out the window collecting his thoughts.

"It was one of those scenes where you want it to stop, and it seems as if it is in slow motion, but I couldn't stop it. When Larry's front wheel hit the pothole, he flipped over the handlebars, and when he landed, his head hit the curb. Man, we all stopped our bikes and ran to Larry. The little boy's mom was screaming and took her son inside so he wouldn't see all the blood. Larry was laying on the ground, all twisted, but he was still breathing. Blood was pouring out of his head, and I could tell he was in bad shape. I ripped off my shirt and wrapped his head while one of the other guys called for help. I held his head and begged God not to let him die. Unfortunately, by the time the paramedics arrived, it was too late. I ah—went off the wagon and other than the funeral, I went missing, until yesterday when I came home. It hit me hard. Larry got himself clean while attending our Bible study and was getting his life back in order. He was working and staying clean. When he died in my arms, I lost it and went back to a few of my old ways. Larry and I served together—we survived the war, and he dies on the street, here on home turf. I was mad, not at God, but life and kept screaming; "Why!"

Then today, I see you go into the water and cried out to God. 'Please God! Please don't let him die. Give me the ability to rescue him! Please give me a chance! Don't let another guy die in my arms!' When I went underwater looking for you, I kept praying to God to give me the strength to help you. I remember feeling through the muddy water, moving branches, and stones out of the way. When I felt your body, I felt a renewed strength and inner peace like I haven't felt in a long time, shoot through my body, and I knew you would make it."

While Christopher was talking, Michael kept wiping his face from the tears that flowed down his cheeks onto his clothes.

Michael shuddered as he thought. *Is that blood or mud on his torn shirt? He has cuts and scrapes all over his arms and hands. It looks like his ribs are bleeding through the shirt.*

"Christopher, are you bleeding?" Michael asked.

"No, I mean, not now. My mom cleaned the cuts and fixed me up. I'm good." Christopher said while gesturing toward his right side with his left hand.

"You-you were injured, saving me and don't give it a second thought. Why? I mean, I still don't understand. You

CHAPTER TWENTY-FOUR

went into the water to save someone you didn't know. I am not sure I could do that. I know that I would do everything I could to protect Abby and my kids, but I am not sure if I could do the same for a stranger."

"Yea, my dad, and grandfather set great examples for me," Christopher said, "but I do what I do because of my Lord and Saviour Jesus Christ. He died for me, and because of what He did, I will see my grandfather and Larry again. When I was a kid at a Bible camp, I asked Christ to save me, but I didn't always walk in faith, and when I started attending the Bible study in town, I gained a new understanding but--. After Larry died, I was shaken, and the night before last, I rededicated my life to Christ, asking Him to use me. To use me in a renewed way. The Bible lesson two nights ago was from the scripture in Luke, 'where much is given, much is required.' Man, when I heard the verse, it wouldn't let go of me. All I kept hearing was I was given a chance at life, and I needed to do something with it and stop wasting it on excuses, booze, and--."

"Another guy in our group—he was riding with us the night Larry died. We didn't serve together, but he played pro football for a few seasons and made more money in a season than most make in a lifetime. The lifestyle got to him. He said his coach kept telling him he needed an accountability partner and not let the money and celebrity status get the best of him. However, he cheated on his wife—they have a little kid together, then he started drinking and more women. One thing led to another, and he quit going to practice, then got cut losing his family and career. It wasn't until one of his buddies suggested that he attend our group that he started to get his life together. Every one of us needs others to help us in our journey. I heard a preacher once say 'no man is an island.' He said it's part of a quote from John Donne, meaning that no one is really self-sufficient. Many like to think that they don't need anyone. But we all need others in our life to keep us accountable, stand with us when life gets tough, and rescue us when needed.

Michael, you were given a second chance at life. You need to decide if you are going to continue trusting in you to run your life or follow God."

Michael looked out the window, and the room was quiet for a few minutes.

I'm scared. Not because of what happened, but how do I fix it? His body shook with a wave of cold chills, but sweat poured off his hands, causing Michael to wipe his hands on the bed sheets over and over.

When Michael looked back, he had a worried look on his face.

"I don't know what to say. I mean—I never felt like this in my life. I could have left Abby alone in the world. Actually, I did leave her alone in the world."

"What do you mean?" Christopher asked.

"For months, I have been working day and night, and she had to deal with the kids, paying bills, and basically she was a single mom that had a paycheck deposited twice per month in the checking account. I was so wrong to let everything get in the way of the commitment I made to her on our wedding day. I don't know. How do I fix it?" Michael asked.

"Actually, you can't," Christopher said.

"Really? I thought you were giving me—hope."

"What I mean is you cannot fix it alone. Life wasn't meant to be lived in a vacuum, nor alone. The Bible talks about going out two by two, and two are better than one, and in the military, we were taught to use the buddy system. We never cleared a room on our own, nor did we go into town alone. Everything we did was with a buddy. Even the sniper had a scout. There is an old saying that we say. 'I've got your six.' I think it originated after World War I,

CHAPTER TWENTY-FOUR

meaning I have your six o'clock or the back of the plane. In today's terms, I have your back.

"First, living life without God is foolish, and for us guys, living life without other guys to hold us accountable is like going into battle without a plan or weapons. There will be loss of life and too often by our own hands."

Michael responded, "I don't know what to say—or do. It all is so much to handle and think about. I don't have the strength like you. I mean—you, your family, the other people. You are different than me. I—I don't know."

"Michael, humbling yourself is tough, and admitting that we cannot do life alone is challenging. You experienced first-hand that without others in your life, you wouldn't be here. One of the best parts about God is free will. It is your choice."

"You are correct, I need to talk to Abby. I—this is a lot to absorb. I ah—" Michael stumbled over his words.

"I understand. There is no pressure from us to you. We will continue to love you and walk with you in life. If you ever want to talk, please call my dad or me. Actually, any one of us. We are here for you. I felt in my heart that I couldn't leave without talking to you alone." Christopher wrote his number on a pad of paper. "This is my mobile number. I am serious. We will talk to you anytime, day or night."

Taking the paper, Michael stared at it for a very long silent minute. "Thank you! I will never forget you, and I owe you more than my life."

Christopher got up from his chair and put it near the wall in its original place, then shook Michael's outstretched hand.

As he was leaving, Christopher said, "Please keep in touch. I am positive God has a plan for your life, and He put me in your path to tell you that His purpose for your life is far greater than you can imagine."

A few minutes later, Abby came back into the room, and Michael recapped what he learned from Christopher.

"There is so much to think about and take in. I had a thought. When you think about everyone we met, there are people from all walks of life and multiple generations. From Zoe to Nana and every age in between. It is almost unbelievable. I wish we could stay longer, but we need to get home, and we have a journey in front of us." Michael said.

Ginnie knocked, paused a few seconds, and opened the door.

"I have the release papers and scripts from Doc. Plus a note if you need anything for work showing you saw a doctor for your injuries. If you are ready, Dan and I will take you back to the cottage. I am sure you are anxious to get home and see your children."

"Yes, we need to get home. I will text my aunt and tell her we will be there in a few hours," Abby said.

CHAPTER TWENTY-FIVE

The ride from Doc's office to the house was quiet except for the uplifting music playing from Zoe's smartphone via Officer Dan's speakers. It seemed as if everyone in the vehicle wanted to give the other time to reflect on the day and for Michael and Abby, the extended weekend.

Upon arriving at the house, Zoe gave both Abby and Michael a hug then quickly exited the vehicle knowing that if she lingered too long, the tears would flow. As she reached the porch, she looked over her shoulder and in her best southern accent said, "Y'all, come back now, ya hear!"

They all chuckled, and a few tears flowed from Abby and Michael's eyes as reality hit. Time to say goodbye for now.

When they reached the cottage, Officer Dan parked the vehicle. They all got out and stood without talking. The only sounds were those of songbirds and a slight wind moving from the west.

Abby broke the silence. "I cannot tell you how much we appreciate your hospitality, kindness, and openness to us."

Michael added. "I agree, we cannot express our gratitude enough. Officer Dan, the other day you could have just done your job, but you showed me, a stranger, kindness. The kindness that I haven't experienced since—since I was a child. I was in a dark place and was drowning in life, and this weekend I nearly drowned physically. Your son,—risked his life for me. Obviously, it runs in the DNA of your family."

Michael paused to gather his thoughts, and in the silence, soft sobs came from Ginnie. Her shoulders lifted in rhythm as she cried. Simultaneously, Officer Dan and Abby hugged Ginnie from the side.

"There is something about Christopher that is unlike other soldiers I met," Michael explained. He is more than a gentle giant. His words, mannerisms, and spirit were—is different—unique. His arms are larger than some people's thighs yet, he doesn't intimidate with his size. I am sure you know that we talked and what he said to me made a profound impact. We never did religion, and I don't know what to say but thank you, and I will call you soon."

"At the times of his greatest despair, He always knew that God is more than able to get him through and into the light," Ginnie said.

"Has Christopher struggled, yes, but—as you said, his spirit is strong, not by his strength, but with the strength given to him from The Lord," said Ginnie softly. She wiped the tears from her eyes and turned away.

Officer Dan continued for Ginnie. "The two of you experienced a miracle. A new beginning. Michael, you were given a second chance at life. I am not big into speeches, and none of us are into religion. I am more of the doing and guiding type. You need to make a choice. Actually, many choices. Don't waste the second chance The Lord provided you today. My son was just a vessel, just like my dad was a vessel to give Zoe a second chance at life. Christopher was willing to lay down his life for your life, but neither of you lost your life and other than a few bruises, you are okay. Please come back with your children, and we will talk more. None of us here do what we do in our own strength. Take your time getting your things together, but I wouldn't wait too long, I smell a storm brewing in the west, and no doubt your kids are anxious to see the two of you."

They all hugged then Michael and Abby went into the cabin to gather their belongings and do some quick cleaning. After removing some of her things from one of

CHAPTER TWENTY-FIVE

the nightstands, she noticed an etching in bronze that read. 'Seek ye the LORD while he may be found, call ye upon him while he is near.' Isaiah 55:6

On the corner of the nightstand was a small tablet and pen. "We should leave a note," said Abby.

"Yes, and Officer Dan mentioned that Zoe cleans the cabin. We need to bless her with a few pictures that I have in my wallet," Michael said.

"Pictures, in your wallet?" Abby asked.

"Yes, I am thinking we leave her a picture of Hamilton and Jackson," Michael said as he removed two twenties and a ten from his wallet and placed them on the nightstand.

"Do you have a picture of Grant? That would be nice too."

"No, but that would be nice. Next time."

"Wait! I think I have a picture of Grant. We don't want anyone to think we took her for granted." Abby said as she laughed at her joke and placed the fifty on the other money.

"Hmm, did you read that in a magazine too?" Michael asked.

"No! Silly! I made it up just now!" Abby said.

"I couldn't tell." Michael rolled his eyes.

Abby and Michael wrote a note to Zoe. 'Thank you for your inspiration and encouragement. You are an amazing young woman, and your kindness and spirit are contagious. We cannot wait until we bring our children to meet you, an example of a person we would like them to become when they grow up. Please accept this gift to help you in your future journeys and adventures. Love Abby & Michael.'

The trip went fast as Abby and Michael talked about the weekend with a new love and filled in parts that the other didn't know. They kept commenting on the generosity and kindness from everyone they met. Michael kept going back to what Christopher told him and how people came out of nowhere for the rescue effort.

A few minutes before arriving at their house, Abby sent a text to her aunt that they were close. As they pulled into their driveway and opened their doors, the night's silence was broken with screams of joy, 'Mommy! Daddy! You're home!' The first to reach them was their ten-year-old son followed seconds later by their two daughters. All three jumped into the air for their parents to catch them with the simplest of faith, which too often only children possess.

Abby and Michael held the three of them so tight that they all said in unison, "We can't breathe!" They rolled on the ground, laughing even as the excitement of the moment wore off, and the pain from Michael's injuries kicked in. Neither wanted this moment to end. Michael got up off the ground and went to Abby's aunt first and gave her a big hug thanking her aunt and uncle over and over for the time they spent with the kids. They promised that they would sit down and tell them about the weekend and fill them in when they had a few days to regroup and recover.

Michael said, almost to himself, "We will tell you all about this weekend. Hmmm, I need to write this down. I don't want to forget any of it. The weekend is almost unbelievable. Maybe—maybe I should write a book? Yea, I need to write all of this down for others to know that there are people in the world who are kind and will walk with you on this journey called life."

CHAPTER TWENTY-SIX

After putting the children to bed, Michael was the first to go to their bedroom. Upon opening the door, the closed up smell from Abby being ill, hit him like a punch from a heavyweight boxer. "Wow! What died in here? It smells worse than some of those bars a few of us visited when in college."

Pulling the door closed, he turned to find Abby in the hallway with an embarrassed look and playing with her hair. "Um, yea. It was rough a few nights ago."

Pulling her tight to him, Michael whispered in Abby's ear. "I am here for you. We will use the guest bedroom to get some much-needed rest."

Waking in pain and with guarded movements, Michael rolled left toward the alarm clock and noticed it was 3:30 AM. Wincing with every move, he turned toward Abby, moved her hair slightly then kissed her cheek. The soft light from the street light bathed her face and hair, creating a radiant look. He smiled, then rolled out of bed. When his left foot touched the floor, needle-like pain stabbed his ankle, and he almost did a face plant into the wall that was only a few feet from the bed, as the searing pain shot up his leg. *Where did I put that walking boot, where is my phone?*

Navigating his way out of the guest suite and attempting to be quiet, he looked in on the children, smiling, then went to the main bath to shower. When he entered it, he was reminded that it needed to be cleaned and after fifteen minutes of searching through various closets found cleaning supplies and did a fair job cleaning up Abby's mess. After tossing the towels on the floor, he took a long shower letting the hot water run off his body, feeling some of the pain dissipate from his ribs and shoulders.

Having a difficult time putting his shirt on without help, he decided to wait until Abby was awake and ask for assistance.

Not one to usually do the laundry and unsure what to do, but in an attempt to help Abby, while using his better arm, he gathered the towels and sheets from the bed and stuffed them in the washer. Hoping for the best, he poured half of the bottle of detergent into the machine before closing the lid and turning it on.

After finding his work phone, he went to the study to email his boss to inform him that he needed a few sick days to recover from the injuries. Additionally, he wanted to spend needed time with Abby and wanted to do something he had not done in a long time. Have a meal with his family, and he would start with breakfast. As someone who always worked, even on the weekends, a real breakfast was rare, and a family dinner did not exist with him included.

However, when he turned on his work phone, he was greeted with emails and a seemingly endless number of voice messages from his boss and peers from work. All weekend they had attempted to contact him for an emergency meeting. He listened to a few voice messages and read multiple emails. He listened to one voice mail from his boss screaming at him, demanding to know where he was and why he was not returning his emails or calls.

Yea, like I want to call you back this morning. Where is the note from Doc? Where are the extra pills and prescriptions?

With his phone in hand, Michael went back into their bathroom and stood in front of the mirror. *What did Robbie tell him?*

Closing his eyes, Michael thought back to his conversation with Robbie. He said he had daily conversations with himself in the mirror. 'The time you are spending, is it

CHAPTER TWENTY-SIX

time well spent and knowing that you cannot get the time back, are you a good steward of TIME?'

Wincing, he examined his left side, all battered and bruised. *I wonder if this is how a punching bag feels the day after the champ works out.*

> "... are you a good steward of your TIME?"

Lifting the phone, he took a close-up picture of his ribs and shoulders in the mirror and an image of Doc's note. Standing in front of the mirror, he looked at himself and pointed a finger to the man in the mirror saying aloud. "You will make a decision for your family and you! Do what is right, not what is easy!"

He opened the email app on his phone and composed a note to his boss Charles Sr., stating he got hurt over the weekend, spent some time in a small health clinic, and needed a few days to heal. Never one to miss a day's work, he added, "I have some sick time coming and need to use it. I will not be at work for a few days. I will call you later in the week."

After staring at the note for a few minutes and the attached images, he hit send knowing his boss would be angry. *I wonder why Charles insists on being called Charles Sr. when he doesn't have a son. Why not Charlie or Charles. Why Charles Sr.?*

Not wanting his administrative assistant, Jada to worry, he sent her a note telling her that he would be off work for a few days, to let his employees and one of his peers Bob know that he would be out of the office.

Seconds after sending the second note, he felt his phone vibrate in his hand. Looking at the screen, he saw it was an email from his boss. *Wow, what was he doing? Was he sitting there waiting for my note?*

Hesitantly, he decided to open the email knowing the response would be curt at a minimum and no doubt demanding. *Would he stand up to his boss and do what was right? Would he make the decision that could—no—would affect his family?*

He opened the email from his boss. 'Unless you are dead, you better be here!' Staring at the email, and then looking into the mirror, he put his phone down and looked up. "God! I need help! What do I do? I can't do this alone! Please help me! Help us!"

With tears running down his face and his vision blurred, he didn't notice the light on his phone flashing nor it vibrating on the vanity top. It wasn't until the smartphone vibrated itself into the sink bowl, making a clattering sound that he snapped out of his trance-like state.

Picking up the phone, through tears in his eyes, he saw he had three missed calls. *God, I hope it is you calling!* However, he knew in his heart who the calls were from—his boss.

Three missed calls from his boss. The first two with no voice messages, but the third call had a voice message, and after listening to a few seconds of his boss screaming, he turned off his phone, put it on the vanity, and washed his face while looking into his bloodshot eyes so swollen that he could barely see his pupils. *Michael, you look bad! If it weren't for the pain in my body, I would wonder if this weekend was real or a dream.*

He heard a sound behind him and still looking into the mirror, he saw Abby sauntering toward him. Sensing something was wrong, she didn't say a word, but wrapped her arms around his waist from behind and held him softly, giving him a gentle kiss on his face.

He put his hands on her hands then turned around, looking at her face to face and kissed her holding her tight. Neither said a word.

After a few minutes of silence, he gave her a brief recap telling her about the voice messages and emails from the weekend, his note to his boss, then subsequent email and voice message.

CHAPTER TWENTY-SIX

Looking around the bedroom, Abby asked, more to herself than Michael. "Where are the bedsheets, pillow covers, comforter, and bed skirt?"

Not hearing her question, Michael said, "Abby, after breakfast, let's take the kids to school, then go get your car from Grandma's house."

Looking into his eyes, she replied, "Really? All of us? Today?"

He replied with a soft yes and sealed the deal with a kiss on the lips.

The kitchen was filled with the smells of pancakes, eggs, and bacon and topped with laughter and giggles from the children.

This was the first time daddy had a meal with them for a long time, and he never took them to school, creating an atmosphere of love and devotion.

The older two went to the same school, but their youngest went to a different school, which was minutes away from the first school.

Before getting out of the car, their youngest, Kendra asked, "Daddy, will you do this—will you do this again tomorrow?" Without waiting for an answer, she jumped out of the car, ran a few steps, stopped, looked back, and blew them a kiss.

Abby and Michael looked at each other and with joy in their eyes, smiled.

CHAPTER TWENTY-SEVEN

"We need to do something with your vehicle. There is a car wash near the coffee shop, and I need my morning coffee. If you buy me a coffee, I will clean out your car. I am surprised the kids had anywhere to sit. Is there anything dead under all that trash in the back seat?" Abby asked as she laughed at her comments.

Pulling out the trash from the seat cushions, she said, "I think I need a hazmat suit! When was the last time you cleaned—"

She stopped when she noticed a magazine sticking out of the back seat cushion. Pulling it out, she realized it was one of those real estate ad magazines that they give away free in stores. It wasn't from any of the stores in their area. It must have fallen out of the bag when they went shopping at the store on their way to Dan and Ginnie's place. Nonchalantly, Abby picked up the magazine and began flipping through it while she slid into the back seat.

"Michael, did you see this magazine? It was in the bag from the place we bought the clothes and other stuff over the weekend."

Michael was attempting to clean out his front seat, but with the pain, he had a difficult time accomplishing anything.

"No? Does it have jokes in it that you intend to use?"

"No, silly! It is one of those free real estate magazines that lists all of the properties for sale in the area!"

"What area? Here?" Michael asked.

CHAPTER TWENTY-SEVEN

"No, we might need to get your head checked out! I think something came loose in it. It is a real estate magazine, and there is a foreclosure going on this week, and I am not good with directions, but I think it is close to Ginnie and Dan's home. Look at this place!" Abby eagerly shoved the magazine in his direction.

Michael looked to where Abby was pointing and stared for a few minutes.

"I know what you are thinking. It needs some TLC—you know Tender Loving Care," Abby said as she chuckled.

"More like Total Lost Cause," Michael commented as he stared at a few black and white photos of an old stone farmhouse with what was once a wraparound porch with grass higher than his waist. In other images, he saw three old barns, and one filled with old cars—some looking as if they were from the fifties and sixties. The ad said it was a bank foreclosure and the sale of the property included twenty acres, house, three barns, and everything within the barns. 'All Sales Final.'

"You need to use our vision plan and get your eyes checked if you see anything in this place!"

A few other pictures showed a small lake in desperate need of a severe cleanup, with a small fishing boat partway submerged in the water with a large hole on its side and his mind began to spin.

Under the address was the date of the auction, which was next weekend, the same as Kendra's birthday. Michael looked at the starting bid for the foreclosure and thought.

God, is this a sign? What do we do?

As Michael was staring at the pictures, Abby's phone rang.

"Hello, Jada? Are you okay? Slow down. Are you crying? Wait, here is Michael." Abby said, tapping the mute button on the phone. "It's Jada; she is hysterical. I couldn't understand what she was saying except—security—take—Michael.

She kept saying, I know Michael is hurt, but I need to talk to him!"

Taking the phone from Abby, Michael turned off the mute button and put the phone to his ear.

"Jada, please slow down—Take a breath—No, it's okay that you called me—Please tell me what happened—Really?—Security came in and with HR marched many people out of the building?—Did they say why?—Hostile takeover?—Who?—I understand.—Where are you?—Home?—Please calm down—Did they hurt you when they escorted you out of the building?—What about Bob? Okay, he wants me to call him—Hold one minute, I need to get a paper and pen. I don't have my phone and cannot remember his number."

Putting the phone on mute, "Abby, do you have a pen and paper in your purse? I am sure I have one in my vehicle, but since I cleaned it, I can't find anything."

Abby looked through the garbage bag and found some paper and a small pencil Michael must have received the only time he golfed since college.

Handing the pencil and paper to Michael, Abby said. "What is going on?"

"I will explain in a few minutes."

Turning the phone off mute, Michael said. "Jada, what is Bob's mobile number...Okay, I have it. Is there anything else that HR or Security told you before you left or did Bob tell you anything? Did Charles say anything to you?—That's okay, it isn't your fault. I will call Bob. When I know something, I will call you. Thank you for calling. Bye." Michael touched the end call button and stared at the phone for a few seconds.

"I need to make a call," Michael said as he slid his hand between the driver's seat and middle console, reaching with his fingers extended, almost touching the floor when he felt what he wanted.

CHAPTER TWENTY-SEVEN

Abby watched him intently, wondering what he was doing. Just as she was about to ask if he needed help, since she could reach under his seat from the back seat easier, she heard him say.

"Got it!" Michael held up a card and put it on the dash directly in front of him.

Watching Michael dial a number, she wondered, whom is he calling? *I hope he isn't calling Charles.*

After a few rings, the call goes to voice mail, and Michael didn't leave a message. Instead, he tapped the end call button and handed the phone back to Abby.

Michael continued making calls that extended into the afternoon. He contacted Bob, then HR and was presented with multiple options. The company he worked for was indeed bought out through a hostile takeover. He was offered the opportunity to stay on with the new company taking on more responsibility with a significant raise or accept a modest severance package. The increase in salary plus potential promotions due to his past performance would help eliminate some of their debt, and with a few other promised perks, many of their financial issues would diminish.

Abby was in the kitchen, preparing dinner when her phone rang.

"Hello? Hi! How are you? Great! Yes, Michael is here and doing better. I am glad you called. I think he called you earlier from this phone; he didn't have his phone when he called. Hold on; I will get him."

Walking to Michael's study, Abby said. "Michael, the phone is for you."

"Who is it?" he asked.

"A friend." Replied Abby as she handed Michael the phone.

Hesitating, Michael said. "Hello?"

"Officer Dan, You don't know how happy I am you called. Yes, I called earlier but hesitated to leave a message. Do you have a few minutes to talk and maybe we can meet? I would like to get your input on a few things."

TO THE READER

Did you ever have a friend that no matter what occurred in life or how long you went between chats, you could pick up the conversation as if there was no passage of time? The friend that you can tell your deepest secrets and always have something to talk about, regardless of the hour?

People will come and go in your life and walk alongside you to help. I hope they will be like the characters in this book. For me, there have been friends, both older and younger. I have gleaned knowledge and guidance from male and female, people of multiple races, creeds, and various walks of life. However, there is only One that helped me understand and appreciate the value of Ecclesiastes 4:9; "Two are better than one; because they have a good reward for their labour."

Although there have been many momentous days in my life, our wedding day, the birth of each child, and every grandchild, the day that stands above all others, is the day when I received Christ as Lord and Saviour of my life.

He knew my good, bad, and indifferent. However, he didn't cast me away. He knew my faults and talents, yet took me as me, not comparing me to others. In a world where comparing is normal, Christ doesn't compare us to others. He gave His life for us without comparison. Most understand that one of the most significant sacrifices is when someone lays down their life in exchange for another person's life. Christ did that for us. (John 15:13)

My words cannot express the deep compassion and care that Christ has and will continue to give me. Although the deep pain of some of my darkest hours has subsided, I will never forget how I cried out, and the Lord not only comforted me but provided help, strength, and healing. His strength, not mine. He has been with me during my most significant trials and magnificent victories. He guided me through to triumphs and provided skills that baffle my mind. Gifts and talents that are not from me but from God.

He has stood with me like no one else, even a brother or sister for He is a friend that will stick closer than a brother. (Proverbs 18:24) He will provide peace in your heart that is not explainable. (Philippians 4:7)

My hope is this book touched your life but more important that if you do not know Jesus Christ as Saviour and Lord of your life, please recognize the need, and take the time today and receive Him into your life. (Romans 10:9)

To receive Christ as your LORD and Saviour, please pray.

"Father, I come to you in the name of Jesus Christ. Thank you for loving us and sending your Son, Jesus Christ to die for our sins. I believe I need a Saviour and that Christ died for my sins. He rose from the dead and is with You in Heaven. I receive Christ as my Lord and Saviour. Guide me in my life, and I know that you will never leave me nor forsake me.

If you received Christ as Saviour or would like to reach out to us, please contact us at:

www.DrFrankKendralla.com

Please remember, "Two are better than one, don't do this thing called life alone!"

www.ingramcontent.com/pod-product-compliance
Lightning Source LLC
LaVergne TN
LVHW011839060526
838200LV00054B/4096